# A STORM IN A TEACUP

In the first of four stories of mystery and intrigue, *A Storm in a Teacup*, Kerry has taken over the running of her aunt's café. After quitting her lousy job and equally lousy relationship with Craig, it seemed the perfect antidote. But her chef, with problems of his own, disrupts the smooth running of the café. Then, 'food inspectors' arrive, and vanish with the week's takings. But Kerry remembers something important about the voice of one of the bogus inspectors . . .

GERALDINE RYAN

# A STORM IN A TEACUP

## AND OTHER STORIES

*Complete and Unabridged*

LINFORD
*Leicester*

First published in Great Britain

First Linford Edition
published 2013

British Library CIP Data

Ryan, Geraldine, *1951 –*
    A storm in a teacup.- -
(Linford mystery library)
1. Detective and mystery stories.
2. Large type books.
I. Title II. Series
823.9′2–dc23

ISBN 978–1–4448–1402–6

F. A. Thorpe (Publishing)
Anstey, Leicestershire

Set by Words & Graphics Ltd.
Anstey, Leicestershire
Printed and bound in Great Britain by
T. J. International Ltd., Padstow, Cornwall

This book is printed on acid-free paper

# A STORM IN A TEACUP

# 1

Kerry wondered if perhaps she should go inside and have a proper look. She might be pleasantly surprised. Either that, or her worst fear — that Aunt Tazie's café had gone seriously downhill from how she remembered it from her childhood — would be confirmed. Take the sign, in the shape of a samovar, for instance. It should have read *Tazie's Tea Rooms*, but now read *Taz Tea Roo*. Then there was the woefully dismal lack of numbers passing through its doors.

Just two people had gone in during the twenty minutes she'd been loitering behind a pillar box, spying on the place. She suspected one of those was Alice Struthers, dragged out of retirement to hold the fort till someone more permanent turned up — ie, herself. The other person was a delivery man, balancing a tray of bread while carefully negotiating his way through a door badly in need of a coat of paint.

Kerry relived the phone call she'd had with her mother just last week.

'Your Aunt Tazie's in a spot of bother with a dodgy hip.'

Straight into it, that was Mum. But then her mother didn't do small talk. Kerry blamed her Russian blood, which both Mum and Aunt Tazie claimed from their aristocratic Russian grandparents who'd fled Moscow to escape persecution from the proletariat.

This inability to exchange pleasantries, coupled with an inclination to dwell on the less joyful side of life, was her mother's curse, so her Irish dad maintained. Thankfully, Kerry had inherited her own sunny nature from him and shared none of her mother's dour pessimism.

Kerry realised she'd been a bit too keen to volunteer her services. But at the time it had seemed like the answer to a desperate prayer — exactly the challenge she needed to wipe Craig's memory from her mind. Well, she'd got her challenge, all right. She'd given Mum her word on the phone, and she couldn't back out now. Her own words rang in her ears, mocking her with their reckless chirpiness. 'Of course I'll help out. I'd be delighted! Isn't that what families are for?'

Besides, she no longer had a job to go back to. The moment she'd given in her notice, her boss, Bob Smiley — now there was a misnomer if ever there was one — had reached for a pen and started drawing up an advert for her successor. Glad to see the back of her, no doubt. They'd never seen eye to eye when it came to sandwich fillings.

'Why can't we experiment?' Kerry made the mistake of demanding, when she'd been in the job less than a week. 'Brighten up people's mundane lives with a bit of variety.'

She suggested lollo rosso. He came right back at her with iceberg. When she pointed out that the only vegetarian options they offered were cheese and egg, bafflingly, he said they did tuna, too. Some people had a wheat allergy, she informed him. Why couldn't they make some sandwiches with gluten-free bread?

If people couldn't eat bread, came his reply, then maybe they'd be better off going to the chippy for their lunch.

In the end she'd given up, although right until the day she buttered her last slice of bread, she'd never quite been able to let go. In her mind, she created exotic combinations for the customers of *Smiley's Sarnies*, enacting the various exchanges with imaginary customers as she applied grated Cheddar and tomato to slices of taste-bud-clenching, factory-sliced white bread.

'So that's one grilled aubergine and tofu on rye, two anchovy with soft-cooked egg on country bread and a ciabatta of smoked ham with frisée and black olives. Any sun-dried tomato pesto with that?'

It passed the time. As did going into raptures about her aunt's business and what a profitable concern it was. If Bob Smiley were standing where she was standing now, then he wouldn't so much as live up to the meaning of his name as surpass it. He'd be laughing his head off!

She, on the other hand, was laughing on the other side of her face. If she hadn't promoted herself to her parents by telling them she managed the sandwich shop instead of telling them the truth, which was that she simply took orders from Bob for a pittance, they might have approached other members of the family more suitably qualified before coming to her.

But even as the thought occurred to her, hot on its heels came the sinking realisation that they probably already had, and these other family members — less gullible than herself — had simply laughed and turned down the opportunity.

The delivery man was coming back outside. Unless a coach party of thirsty, retired people drew up in the moment it took her to cross the road, this was probably a good time to go and introduce herself to Alice Struthers.

'Come on now, Kerry. You can do it. Big smile. Now, off you go and make Aunt Tazie proud,' she said as, looking in both directions she stepped off the pavement.

★ ★ ★

When he opened the industrial-sized dishwasher, blithely assuming it must have reached the end of its cycle, Zoran Petrovic wasn't prepared for it still being full of scummy water and dirty dishes. His discontent, which had been smouldering even while he slept, ratcheted up a few more notches as he took out every plate, glass and piece of cutlery and washed them all by hand. On days like this, he felt just like Dad's old pressure cooker. Unless he got a break soon, he feared the lid would come off and he'd go crazy. The lid finally did come off two hours later when he opened his pay packet and discovered he'd been docked an hour's money.

'You come in late, you lose money,' was how Andreas explained it when Zoran queried it. 'What? You tell me I'm wrong about this?'

Zoran's first instinct was to hit him. In his present state of mind he would have enjoyed nothing more than to lay Andreas clean out. But then he reminded himself that it had only been by refusing to let it show just how much this man was getting to him that he'd managed to cling on to his self-respect all these months.

'OK,' he said, removing his overalls and throwing them down on to the ground. 'You win. Find yourself another gimp. I'm off.'

It was sweet revenge to walk out and leave Andreas with customers who had money he couldn't take off them because he'd lost his chef. He'd done the right thing, holding back from swinging a punch, he told himself as, outside at last, he exchanged fresh air for the stench of animal fat.

The pride he felt from having conquered his baser instincts sustained him only as far as the corner, however. What was he supposed to do now? He couldn't go home because if he did his father would demand an explanation. And since he could never lie to his father that meant he'd have to tell him why he'd walked out.

His father would blame himself, of course. Because, by law, Andreas had been right to dock his pay. On the morning he'd turned up to work late, Zoran had been afraid his father was about to go into one of his black moods. So he'd stayed with him to make sure he was out of bed and, over a breakfast he prepared himself and insisted his father ate, spent time helping him formulate a plan of how to fill the rest of the day most productively till Zoran came home again.

He'd been foolish enough to think that, by confiding in Andreas about some of the things that had happened in his father's life, Andreas might be sympathetic if, occasionally, Zoran got held up at home. It wasn't as if he didn't do the work of two men when he was there, and for the pay of less than one. But Andreas had no concept of family duty. All he understood was profit.

Oh, well, much good may it do him! Zoran felt suddenly foolish, dawdling on the street like a layabout with nothing better to do, while people with a real purpose scurried by, occasionally casting suspicious glances in his direction.

He sighed. All he needed was a chance

to show the world what he could do, to prove he was more than some average Joe, destined to go through life working in a string of low-paid, unskilled jobs just because he had to put his commitment to his father first.

If the opportunity had ever come his way, he would have trained to be a proper chef. He could be working in a big London hotel by now. Or even running his own place. He hated this resentment that occasionally bubbled up towards his father and felt suddenly ashamed of himself. It was for his sake that his father had brought them all to England in the first place — a country that could offer him the opportunities he'd be denied back home.

That had been the idea, anyway. But Fate had played a cruel joke. The family may have fled their war-torn past, but they'd carried the memory of the events they'd left behind and dumped them right in the middle of their new home.

Zoran, a boy when they left, had been the resilient one. But the experiences they'd put all their efforts into shielding their son from had eaten away at the health of both his parents; snatching his mother's life before she'd been in England three years, and beginning to take its toll on his father's mental well-being.

His father didn't choose to have these black moods — they came from nowhere. It was Zoran's duty to look after him, and if the only way he could do that properly was to put his own ambitions to one side, then so be it. His father wouldn't be around for ever and he had years ahead in which to realise his own secret dreams.

Unaccountably, Zoran found himself thinking of his granny, who they'd left behind — dead now, of natural causes, thank God. A brief note of mourning resonated somewhere deep inside him, and the fragrant scent of his granny's apple cake reached his nostrils, magically borne on the urban air, from a time long past. It had been his granny who'd given him his love of food; she was the one he'd run to as a small boy whenever he was in trouble.

He should pull himself together, stop

feeling sorry for himself. The past was over. Looking around, he realised he was standing at a crossroads. He could go left or right. Or cross the road and go straight ahead.

Maybe Granny wasn't all that far away after all, he thought, with a wry smile. Maybe she was trying to tell him something. Which way should he go? He couldn't turn back, that was for sure. He'd done with Andreas and cooking rubbish food he couldn't eat. So, if he couldn't go back, then he must go forward. It had to be better than standing still.

★  ★  ★

Kerry was well aware of the flaws in her nature. That she was gullible was one. Otherwise why would she have allowed herself to be taken in by Craig, in hindsight a man so obviously married that he might just as well have had the word *Wed* tattooed in letters an inch high on his forehead?

Her other main fault was that she

craved affection. Maybe that was to do with always having to work so hard as a child to get a smile out of her mother. It distressed her that Alice Struthers was acting so cool towards her. She'd had a bad working relationship with Smiley at the sandwich shop and she didn't want to repeat the pattern with the woman who'd served in Aunt Tazie's café from the very first day it opened more than twenty-five years ago.

It would have been easier to say Alice was inflexible, like Bob Smiley, and leave it at that. Both of them, for different reasons, hated change. Bob because he lacked imagination and Alice because she'd rather be at home pruning her roses. But Kerry didn't want to start off on the wrong foot with Alice. She wanted her to be as enthusiastic about this new venture as Kerry herself. Unfortunately, enthusiasm counted for very little if you'd never actually managed a business before, which is why she desperately needed to get Alice on her side.

If only she'd stop turning her mouth down and sighing every time Kerry suggested doing something differently. What she needed was an ally. Someone who shared her vision of an exciting new menu and a complete change of decor. And when Zoran Petrovic walked in off the street, asking for a job and then, when he'd been unable to produce references, made such a heartfelt plea for the opportunity to show just what he could do instead, she thought she'd found him.

But now here she was again, once the last customers of the day had left — all three of them — and they'd put up the closed sign, having to justify the decision to take him on. A downright foolish idea, according to Alice.

'What kind of a name is Zoran, anyway?' For a woman of her age she couldn't half get round the tables with a cloth quickly. 'How do you know he's legal?'

'He showed me his passport. It says: *Leave to remain*,' Kerry said. 'He's been here since he was a boy.'

She wished Alice had left her a few tables to clear. She flicked a cloth about to make herself look busy.

'Zoran will reinvigorate this place,' she said, in his defence. 'Have you tasted that apple cake of his?'

'Too much cinnamon in it for my liking,' Alice said. 'And very likely for our regulars, too.'

'Well, I thought it was delicious. Much more exciting than that shop-bought Battenberg.'

'Battenberg's traditional.'

Obviously, as far as Alice was concerned, that was enough to justify its inclusion on the menu. Ditto the toasted teacakes, the scones and the Chorley cakes. Privately, Kerry thought 'traditional' was the reason the place always seemed to be half-empty. People's taste buds had changed since Alice donned her first miniskirt and sipped frothy coffee in the first continental coffee bar to hit her village high street.

The best thing to do in order not to alienate Alice totally, she'd already decided, was to make the changes she wanted and only inform Alice after the event. She'd already switched milk suppliers, because she'd found someone who could deliver much more cheaply than the people Aunt Tazie had been using for the last quarter of a century. She didn't have Alice's experience, but she could add up! It was no wonder this place made no profit.

She made one last attempt to get on Alice's good side. 'Look,' she said, 'you go, Alice. Get the earlier bus. Zoran and me can finish off here.'

But just like every other attempt she'd made to make herself amenable, Alice succeeded in making Kerry feel she'd done something to offend her.

'If that's what you want,' she said dourly, removing her apron.

'Now she thinks I want to get rid of her.' Kerry sighed, as Alice waddled out of the door. There was more to running a business than just mastering the figures, and that was a fact.

★  ★  ★

'There's no milk!'

Zoran was mixing batter for apple-cheese squares, when Alice burst into the kitchen. Zoran frowned as he worked. When he baked, he put his full concentration into it. Baking was like praying, his granny used to say. You had to give it all you'd got or God didn't hear you.

His chocolate hazelnut cake sat cooling on the side. He noticed Alice staring at it.

'Want to try a piece?' he asked 'It's my granny's recipe. Just like my apple-and-cinnamon cake.'

Her eyes narrowed. She continued to eye the cake suspiciously, but her mouth had grown slack. Zoran was satisfied that sooner or later Alice would weaken.

'I haven't got time for cake,' Alice snapped. 'I'm too busy wondering how I'm expected to make tea with no milk.'

'Oh, dear.'

Zoran wasn't one to tell tales out of school. He liked Kerry. She'd done a lot for him, taking him on with no references. Why on earth she'd done it so readily he couldn't imagine, though he rather suspected it was as much to do with her stamping her authority all over Alice as with the lightness of the pastry he'd baked for her, as proof that he really could do the job and was not just bluffing his way in.

'She said something about changing the supplier,' he said. 'She's worked out somewhere we can get it cheaper. I think she pinned the number up on the noticeboard, actually.'

Alice marched over to the noticeboard and seized the offending piece of paper containing the details of the new supplier.

'Milk Magic!' Her voice dripped with contempt. Zoran took a step back, relieved that his mixing bowl stood between Alice's wrath and himself.

Kerry breezed into the kitchen, her eyes bright with that forced enthusiasm that made Zoran wonder what secret unhappiness she was hiding.

When Kerry read the fury in Alice's eyes, she stopped dead.

'What have I done?' she piped up.

Alice's nose twitched. For Kerry's information, she said, her Aunt Tazie had always got her milk from Mr Jones, at the dairy. She got her bread from Browns' bakery and her eggs from the farm down the road. It might be a bit dearer for the consumer but it was how Aunt Tazie liked it.

'It might be the old-style way, but old doesn't always have to mean past it, you know,' she finished by saying.

Kerry hung her head, deeply affected by this ticking off. Zoran couldn't help feeling sorry for her. She stared at the floor, shuffling her feet, obviously thinking hard. Then, like someone struck by inspiration, she slapped her head with the flat of her hand.

'I've been a fool, Alice, and I'm very sorry. Will you forgive me?'

Alice looked disappointed that it had taken so little for Kerry to capitulate, Zoran thought.

'Local produce for local people, of course! But why on earth didn't Aunt Tazie make more of it?'

'Well, I did try to tell her she should advertise it more. But she was a bit stubborn, your auntie,' Alice said. 'Thought you shouldn't have to make things too easy for people. Not that I'm being disloyal.'

'Of course not,' Kerry said. 'Sounds just like my mum.'

She grinned at Alice and Alice almost, though not quite, smiled back at her.

'I'll get on the phone right away, cancel Milk Magic and reinstate Mr Jones. And then I'll make some signs. *Only local seasonal produce used in the making of our tasty cakes and snacks.*'

Then she was gone, leaving Alice and Zoran alone once more.

'Cake, Alice?'

Alice's gaze hovered over the chocolate hazelnut cake.

'Your granny's recipe, did you say?'

'That's right.'

'In that case,' Alice said, 'I'll give it a go.'

★ ★ ★

The clock had just struck five-thirty and Kerry, who'd sent the others home and put up the closed sign, was alone in the café. She felt quite cheerful as she counted the week's takings. Three weeks in, they weren't exactly bursting at the seams with customers, but word was spreading and business was definitely picking up.

She had Zoran's delicious cakes to thank for that, though Alice, too, was definitely more on board these days since Kerry had stopped riding roughshod over her. The knock at the door surprised her. The sign clearly said they closed at five o'clock. She wondered if her mum had decided to pop by and see how she was doing. It was like her to turn up unexpectedly and then complain because there was no one in. But this time she was. She bundled up the last wodge of tenners and slapped them down on the counter.

'Just coming!' she cried out, bustling towards the door. 'Oh!'

It was a woman all right, but not her mother. About forty, smart, very dark hair and quite a bit of make-up, and carrying a clipboard. Kerry didn't like the look of this. It looked official.

'Food inspectors.'

The woman flashed some ID at her, but Kerry was too thrown to read it properly. The woman said something about Section bla-bla-bla of the yadda-yadda-yadda act of nineteen something, following it with a bit about having the right to enter premises where food was served without giving notification. It was a bit like having your rights read, Kerry thought.

Oh, why had she sent Alice home? She'd have known what to do. The woman had a man with her, all togged up in a white suit, hairnet and wellies, and a mask of the type she'd seen people who were worried about getting swine flu wearing on the news.

'You'd better come in,' Kerry said, praying to God that Zoran had scrubbed the kitchen to within an inch of its culinary life.

'I'll just slip my overalls on if that's OK,' the woman said. 'My colleague will make a start in the kitchen.'

'What is it you're looking for, exactly?'

Kerry followed the man around as he poked about in corners and opened cupboards. She didn't get much out of him other than something that sounded like 'wisteria'.

Since it was obvious he wasn't exactly the chatty type, she decided to seek out his colleague, who was by the till making notes on her clipboard.

'Is it good?' Kerry wanted to know.

'Our report will arrive within five days, according to regulations,' the woman said. 'But while you're here, I need to ask you to find your certificate.'

Kerry's mind went blank. The only certificates she had were her GCSEs and her swimming ones. The 'wisteria' man came out of the kitchen, his overalls rustling as he walked.

'Food hygiene certificate. Form 456. Evidence that you passed the inspection last time.'

Kerry racked her brain.

'They may be in a drawer somewhere,' the woman said helpfully.

'Right,' Kerry said. 'What drawer?' she wondered.

'I suggest you go and look for them,' the woman said, after a moment had passed, during which time Kerry just stood there looking clueless.

'I'll be right back with it,' she said. 'You

just wait here and carry on doing what you were doing.'

The obvious thing to do, she decided, once she'd fled back into the kitchen and ransacked a few drawers, all to no avail, was to phone Alice. She'd know where this certificate was if anyone did.

But when Alice finally got round to answering the phone, she hadn't got a clue what she was talking about.

'Who did they say they were?' she asked.

'Food inspectors,' Kerry said. 'They want to see something called Form 456.'

The line went ominously quiet for a few seconds. Then Alice spoke again.

'Is there anyone there with you, Kerry?' Alice said.

'No. Just me and the food inspectors.'

'Food inspectors don't inspect premises when they're closed, Kerry. And there's no such thing as a Form 456.'

Kerry moved the phone away from her ear. From the café salon came no sound. Not even the rustling of overalls or the squelch of wellies.

'I'll be right back,' she said.

It was with a feeling of dread that Kerry, on leaden feet, went through to the salon.

'Hello,' she quaked. 'Anyone there?'

The only reply she got was the humming of the fridge. It looked like her visitors had fled. Taking every single penny of the money they'd made that week with them.

# 2

'Don't be too hard on yourself, dear.'

Alice set down the tray and took her seat next to a whey-faced, teary-eyed Kerry. Everyone was being so kind. She'd let slip to Zoran that she had a weakness for carrot cake and, bless him, here was a piece, mouth-wateringly moist and expertly frosted with cream cheese, sitting on a white plate, just begging to be eaten. He must have asked Alice to bring it in just before he'd gone home.

Zoran himself was keeping out of her way. Leaving her to lick her wounds in private, Kerry thought, which was very tactful of him. Alice had no such scruples. Funnily enough, though, her presence didn't chafe half as much as she'd imagined it would. She'd thought the older woman would be bound to see the burglary as Kerry's own stupid fault — proof, should any more be needed, that she wasn't fit to stand in her Aunt

27

Tazie's shoes. Instead, here she was, mothering her.

'Even the police said how clever they'd been, pretending to be food inspectors.'

Alice shook her head at the cheek of it and poured two cups of hot, brown tea.

'They wouldn't have got past you, though, would they?'

Alice didn't deny this. But she didn't exactly wallow in the truth of Kerry's remark either.

'When you get to my age you can see most things coming,' she said.

'It's the other way with me.' Kerry gulped her tea. 'People see *me* coming. Burglars, men, you name it. Gullible should be my middle name.'

'Well, we've all been foolish where men are concerned.'

Kerry was intrigued by Alice's enigmatic words. Could it be that beneath the wrinkled, roly-poly exterior, there beat the heart of a woman who'd known both love and betrayal, just as she'd done?

She felt a sudden terrible ache deep inside and an urgent desire to confide in someone. If only she felt stronger, she wouldn't be so pathetically needy. She'd tried to be strong, God only knew, throwing all her energies into making the café work. But her strength was a delusion — a house built of straw. All it had taken was for two big bad wolves to huff and puff until they'd blown it down, leaving her — foolish, delusional little piggy that she was — standing alone in the middle of the rubble.

'It's not just the burglary, is it?' Alice said. 'I know you've already spoken to the insurance people and they're pretty sure your claim will go through.'

When Kerry failed to reply, Alice drained her cup then rose to put the kettle on again.

'I've only an empty house to go home to,' she said. 'So if you want to talk about what's really troubling you, I don't mind listening.'

So it was that Kerry found herself telling Alice all about Craig. From their first meeting — she'd dropped into the Station Hotel, in desperate need of strong liquor after putting her demanding mother on a train — and there he was, leaning against the bar, self-consciously toying with a bottle of Italian beer, like a man unused to being alone. A more experienced woman would immediately have worked out that that was because, generally speaking, he wasn't.

It was Kerry who'd made the first move, she told Alice, though at the time she hadn't thought of her friendly grin as a move at all — it was her nature to smile at strangers, particularly if they looked down in the dumps.

He was on business, a stranger to the town. She made him laugh with her embroidered version of the shopping trip she'd just endured with her mother. When he asked her if she knew of anywhere nice to eat, it seemed the most natural thing in the world to suggest they ate together.

'Three months it lasted. Phone calls, texts, you know. We'd meet at the hotel, whenever he was in town on business. I was always waiting, it seemed.' Kerry laughed nervously. 'A complete giveaway, I suppose. But I was far too besotted to see the signs.'

'Signs? What signs?'

Kerry dropped her gaze to the ground. 'Married signs,' she said.

When she raised her eyes again, nervously searching Alice's face for some trace of disapproval, she found none. It appeared Alice was unshockable. Encouraged, she continued.

'I think I already knew the truth before I discovered it,' she said. 'I wasn't to ring him in the evenings, unless it was by arrangement. He couldn't give me an address because he was sofa-surfing while he looked for something permanent. All stuff to make you suspicious.'

'Sofa-surfing?' Alice blinked uncomprehendingly.

'Sleeping at the houses of different friends.'

'I see.'

'Then there was this thing he did. Rolling his thumb over the place his wedding ring would be, if he'd been wearing one.'

'Ah.'

'I knew he lived in Alebury. He left a ticket lying around. By then, I was on the verge of searching through his pockets for evidence of what I already thought I knew. What stopped me was I didn't know what I'd do if I found out my suspicions were correct.'

Alice reached out and patted Kerry's hand. 'You loved him, didn't you?' she said. 'Stands to reason you didn't want to find out he belonged to someone else.'

Kerry blinked back a tear.

'I went there a couple of times on my days off. Stupid, I know. Kept hoping I might bump into him and he'd tell me how amazing it was to see me and take me in his arms and tell me he couldn't stand to be away from me for another minute.'

'That didn't happen, though, am I right?'

'One day I was on the bus going back to the station to catch my train home. The traffic was slow because it was round about four o'clock. School-run time. My bus stopped at the lights. We were in the inside lane. A four by four drew up next to us, driven by a woman. Blonde, pretty. Older than me. Two little girls in the back in school uniform.'

She clasped her hands in her lap. It was if it had happened yesterday.

'There was someone in the passenger seat. I could see his knees and his hands, the top of his head but not much else at first. They were having a conversation — that much was clear. Of course, I couldn't hear what was being said. Something made them laugh, though. She grinned at him and he put his hand on her knee.'

She'd seen him turn round, lean forward as he passed something over to one of his daughters, a book, a toy, she couldn't remember which, before ruffling the hair of the other.

'You don't need to say any more, Kerry,' Alice said. 'The fact that he was in the car with his wife and children says it all.'

'I was such a fool, Alice.'

'Not enough of one to still be carrying on with it, though.'

'He didn't put up much of a fight when I said we were finished,' Kerry said. 'And I guess that still hurts my pride.'

'I don't know about pride. In my

experience, it's humiliation that a woman feels in those circumstances.'

Kerry shot Alice a guarded look.

'Oh, yes. I've had my own experience of married men,' she said. 'Had my heart broken just like you, dear.'

'Oh, Alice. I'm very sorry.'

'Don't be. It was a long time ago.'

'There's been no one else?'

Alice laughed. 'My trouble was I let it go on for too long. Believed his story about being married to an invalid. Of course, he couldn't leave her, poor woman. Twenty-five years I wasted on that one.'

'What happened in the end?'

'She got better,' Alice said. 'And I got old. Guess which one he ended up with?'

Alice's expression was one of resignation. 'If you ask me, you did a very wise thing finishing with your young man. There's plenty of unmarried fish in the sea for someone as young and pretty as you are.'

Kerry grinned. She felt suddenly so much better.

'How about going halves with me on

that carrot cake?' she said.

Alice eyed it speculatively.

'You could do worse than Zoran, you know,' she said.

Kerry blushed. 'Don't be daft,' she said. 'I'm not in the market.'

Alice picked up a knife and cut the piece of cake in half. 'Don't leave it too late before you decide you are, that's all,' she said. 'Any man who can bake cakes as good as this one is too much of a catch to be allowed to get away.'

* * *

'I've got a brilliant idea!'

Alice and Zoran stopped what they were doing — companionably skinning hazelnuts in a rhythmic two-step to the accompaniment of the whirring fan oven and the rumbling dishwasher.

'There's no need to look like that.' Their covert exchange of glances hadn't gone unnoticed. 'You'll like it, I promise you.'

'Go on then. Hit me,' Alice said.

'Well,' Kerry said. 'You know how we

don't open Sundays or Mondays.'

'Because we already work a forty-hour week, you mean?'

Kerry was hard put to discover any trace of irony in Alice's intonation, but she knew when she was being got at. Zoran's lips twitched imperceptibly but he kept his eyes on his task. He was a good worker, was Zoran, but as soon as Kerry tried to involve him in any discussion about how to get more customers in, he seemed to withdraw. She put it down to lack of ambition.

'Thing is, although business is starting to pick up, I still think we could do more.'

'What sort of more?' Alice was interested, in spite of herself.

'I'd really like to try opening on a couple of evenings. For dinner, you know. Nothing too fancy. Three starters, choice of two meat and two fish dishes, one vegetarian and a maximum of three puddings.'

It was better to come out with it all at once, she'd already decided. Zoran had stopped shelling nuts and had strolled over to the other end of the room to check something in the oven. She hoped it wasn't apple cake. Any more of it and she'd be on the menu herself as a dumpling.

'We've got no booze licence,' Alice said.

'We charge corkage,' Kerry came back. 'Thirty pence to open a bottle of wine. Even if it's a screw top. What's not to like?'

Alice nibbled a few hazelnuts while she thought it over. One day, Kerry would speak to her about eating the profits, but probably not just yet. Not till they were making a profit, anyway.

'What do you think, Alice?'

'It's not what *I* think.' Alice nodded her head imperceptibly in Zoran's direction. While they'd been talking, he'd opened the back door and slipped outside. 'You can't open without a chef, and from where I'm standing it looks like Zoran's none too keen to do overtime.'

Kerry chewed over Alice's words. It was true he did seem to shoot off on the dot of five.

'I'll speak to him,' she said. 'And I'll try not to be so intimidating.'

'Good,' Alice said. 'You're learning.'

Zoran was sitting on the back step, clasping his knees and staring out at a vista of bins.

'Looks quite pretty, don't you think? Blue for plastic, green for vegetable waste. They should have a red one, though. Black's so drab.' Kerry knew she was gabbling but couldn't seem to stop.

Zoran shifted position slightly. He seemed a long way off, Kerry thought. It was a relief when he spoke.

'I love working here, Kerry,' he said. 'I like the customers, and how you trust me to do things my way. I like the way the kitchen smells. I like the fact that I can be certain the equipment won't break down. And I like the hours.'

'Ah.'

There was really no other answer to this.

'Well, I guess we'll just have to forget it, then,' she said. 'I really don't fancy hiring another chef. And if you don't want the extra hours — '

Zoran turned to face her.

'I know what it must look like to you,'

he said. 'And in another life — well — I'd be here all day and every day, experimenting with new dishes, helping you look for local suppliers. But I have to consider my father.'

'Your father? Is he an invalid?'

'Sometimes it feels like that,' Zoran said sadly.

Kerry sat quietly and waited for Zoran to gather himself together. Haltingly at first, then gradually gathering confidence, he told her all about his father's war-torn past and flight for freedom and the sudden loss of his wife, Zoran's mother, just as a new opportunity to start again had seemed within touching distance, leaving him prone to such deep depressions that Zoran didn't feel able to risk being too far away from him for long.

'It's the unpredictability of his moods,' he said, once he'd got to the end. 'There are days when he's full of energy, just as I remember him. But on other days . . . I need to be at hand, you know? I owe him so much.'

Kerry could have kicked herself for the way she'd misread Zoran. He was no clock-watcher. How could she have thought so? It was plain to see just how dedicated a chef he was.

Recently she'd found herself watching him, poring over the pages of a cookery book, his brow furrowed as he read. Or deftly mixing ingredients for a cake, adding a pinch of this and a sprinkle of that. He was a conjuror where food was concerned. But a juggler in life.

'Funny,' she said. 'I heard about that war. Saw it on the news and everything. I was only a kid at the time, but I remember thinking, these people look just like us. It could have been my family. We were lucky, that's all, fetching up when we did and where we did.'

Zoran nodded. They sat in silence for a while, Zoran deep in thought, and Kerry trying to guess what those thoughts might be.

'War hits people differently,' he said, after a while. 'Some grab the opportunity for a new start. They're happy to take what job they can, content to live wherever they're housed, because at the end of the day they've got their freedom.

My dad, though . . . ' He shook his head despairingly.

'Maybe if your mum hadn't passed away . . . '

He smiled at her. 'Maybe.'

'I'd like to meet him,' she said, suddenly upbeat. Too much introspection gave her a headache. Any more on top of her little chat with Alice and she'd be getting a migraine.

'You would?' He looked at her, surprised.

'Of course. Why not? I like meeting new people. I'm nosy.'

Zoran considered it. 'Well,' he said, 'we don't get many visitors. His old compatriots come round occasionally. They fill the flat with cigarette smoke, drink too much and start reminiscing.'

'Maybe that's the problem,' Kerry said. 'Too much living in the past and not enough living in the present.'

'You might be right,' he said. He gripped his knees in a decisive movement and pulled himself upright. 'Come for supper tomorrow night. Short notice, but any longer and I know just what will happen. He'll work himself up into such a state he'll convince himself it's the Queen who's coming to visit.'

'You're on,' Kerry said. 'I'll wear my tiara.'

★ ★ ★

At some earlier stage of the night, Kerry must have tumbled deep into an unfathomable well of sleep. Now she came thrusting upwards, dizzy with the suddenness of waking, startled by the green digits on her bedside clock that read 3:43 and by the moonlight that flooded her room.

Odd that she should see the moon — why hadn't she closed her curtains before climbing into bed? Although, actually, she didn't remember much about getting into bed at all. Did she fall out of a taxi? That was a possibility.

No, a lift — that was it. And a bit of a tussle with her handbag, which wouldn't reveal in which of its many pockets it was hiding her key. Zoran found it in the end, let her in and left her at the door.

What was it he said before he said goodbye? *Cheese and pickle on white bread, no butter.* Surely not! Drink water. That was it. Or you'll have the mother of all hangovers in the morning. Oh, why hadn't she listened to him?

A silver streak of light illuminated her discarded clothes, half on, half off the chair; skirt, top, bra, tights all hanging on to each other in a drunken embrace. She had no memory of taking her clothes off at all. Fleetingly, she wondered where on earth her shoes were. She sighed. Oh, well, it must have been a good night. But it promised to be a dreadful morning.

Zoran had warned her about his father's slivovitz, too. She groaned and put her hand to her head, willing herself to get up and follow his advice about the water, albeit belatedly. But she found herself simply unable to move.

Gradually, slivers of memory chinked against each other, sparking off new ones. Zoran had been nervous when he opened the door, apologising for the smallness of the flat, for the glasses that didn't match, for the fact that he was going to have to rush off back to the kitchen right away.

'Off you go, then,' his father — whom Zoran introduced as Mehmet — had teased. 'Allow me to look after our charming guest.'

Kerry had rarely come across such old-fashioned manners before. Coupled with the waistcoat and the well-polished shoes, and his habit of bowing each time he addressed her, he was like something from a time gone by. His sweet manner made her giggle and she kept getting the urge to pull her dress over her knees, as if to prove to Mehmet that she might act like a tomboy but at heart she was a proper lady.

'I don't know who Zoran thinks I am,' she said, sipping the first of the glasses of slivovitz that he proffered throughout the evening. 'He should come to my flat. Your place is a palace in comparison.'

And she wasn't fibbing either. The flat was a delight. Exotic. Foreign. Full of warmth and colour and bizarre-looking artefacts haphazardly placed yet — oddly — managing successfully to lend an air of the exotic to every corner.

'You are his employer,' Mehmet said. 'He thinks very highly of you. More than that, you are his saviour.'

'Is that what he says?' she squeaked, holding her glass out for a refill. She was nervous and when she was nervous, she drank.

'He doesn't have to say it, young lady,' Mehmet said, obligingly refilling her glass before topping up his own. 'I am his father. I hear him singing in the bathroom in the morning before he goes to work and I see how the strain and the stress have gone from his face since he started this new job. And these things — they are all down to you.'

Kerry felt light-headed from such a compliment. And from the alcohol, too, undoubtedly. For the rest of the evening, throughout the delicious meal, and the laughter and the dancing and singing that followed — thanks to more slivovitz — she cherished Mehmet's words. She didn't believe she'd ever heard anything so complimentary in all her life.

'I never got a chance,' she said, when Zoran, who, after one glass, had swapped the slivovitz for water, had disappeared into the kitchen again to make coffee, 'to say that Zoran is my saviour, too. Or rather, my aunt's.'

'He told me that your aunt is in poor health at the moment. She must be very proud of how much you're doing to turn her business round.'

'Couldn't do it without Zoran,' she said, wagging her finger randomly. 'Only wish I could go a step further and open in the evening. A bistro. What do you think, Mehmet? Somewhere for the younger set to come for a delicious meal rustled up by a first-rate chef.'

'Is this your dream?'

'A dream that will never be fulfilled, unfortunately,' Kerry said, as Zoran entered with the coffee.

She must have dropped off then, drowned in slivovitz. She heard the two men talking in a language she couldn't understand. *Cheese and pickle on white bread, no butter.* No, of course not, that was ridiculous.

Not exactly arguing, but talking quickly backwards and forwards, like something being explained and something denied, and then more staccato backwards and forwards until the voices grew calmer and everything seemed to be resolved. That must have been shortly before Zoran had put her in his rickety old car and driven her back home.

Oh, wait! There was something else. At the door. Something besides Zoran urging her to drink water before she went to bed. *You may get your wish, after all*, he said. *What?* she'd said. *What? Tell me.*

But he'd shaken his head. *Tell you tomorrow*, he said, *when you're sober and when I can be sure he means it*. He'd been grinning, walking backwards to his car with that easy, fluid gait of his. Oh, well, whatever it was he had to be so excited about, she'd find out tomorrow. Or maybe that was today.

*Cheese and pickle on . . .* What was that phrase playing and replaying in her head? A customer, that was it, at the sandwich shop. Every day at midday, he'd come in for the same old stupid sandwich.

It was no use. If she was going to be

able to do her job tomorrow, she was going to have to sort her head out. Funny old thing, memory, she mused, as she ran the tap till the water came out icy cold. How it crept up on you. Snippets of conversation half-remembered. Voices. Accents.

And then she stood stock-still, too shocked even to turn off the tap so that water spilled over the sides of the glass soaking her hand. *Cheese and pickle on white bread, no butter.* The words were different but the voice had been the same.

The food inspector. The man in the white coat and the mask. One half of the team who'd robbed her of a week's takings.

'I am so on to you,' she muttered, draining the glass of water until not a drop was left and banging it down hard on the side of the sink.

# 3

From the look of the sandwich display, Smiley's Sarnies hadn't changed. They were still anaesthetising the customer's palates with mousetrap cheese and woolly tomatoes on plastic bread, Kerry noticed.

There was a new girl, though. Rosy-cheeked and eager looking, she stepped forward to greet Kerry warmly. Bob Smiley was in the back, she said, when Kerry asked to see him, but would be out any minute.

'Like it here, do you?' Kerry asked to pass the time.

The girl shrugged. 'Beggars can't be choosers.' Then she blushed, afraid, perhaps, that she'd given Kerry the impression of disloyalty to the man who paid her wages. For that, Kerry decided she liked this girl very much.

'Now then, I hope you haven't come for your job back.'

Bob Smiley came bustling into the

front of the shop, wiping his hands on his apron. Kerry reminded herself to decline should he offer to rustle up a sandwich for her to take out.

'No thanks, Bob. I'm quite happy where I am,' she said.

Which she was. For the first time tonight they were opening as Tazie's Bistro — and to a full house. It would be a three-course, recession-busting dinner. Seventeen pounds including a glass of wine. Everyone was on board. Even Zoran's dad, who said he'd do anything he could to help get them off to a grand start.

*No job too lowly* had been his exact words. Alice still couldn't get over them. *A man as fine as that,* she'd said, *mucking in for peanuts with the rest of us.* Smitten, without a doubt.

Kerry chose to ignore the peanuts remark, though she could have mentioned that she paid well above the minimum wage — if you counted tips. When it came to correcting Alice, she'd be the first to admit she was a coward.

She turned her attention back to Bob.

'I do need your help to track someone down though,' she said.

It was almost a week later when the full significance of those words had crept into her memory through a sleepy, drunken haze — *cheese and pickle on white bread, no butter.*

Her immediate reaction had been to ring Zoran, who'd been remarkably unfazed at being dragged out of bed in the early hours. He could have put her wild ramblings down to the slivovitz but instead he said it sounded like a definite lead and they'd talk about it further the next day.

The conclusion they'd reached was that Kerry should call on her ex-boss and ask if he could shed any light on the identity of the man who, a couple of times every week, according to Kerry's memory, uttered these words over the counter at Smiley's Sarnies. In the exact same voice as the one that belonged to one half of the duo who'd robbed Kerry of a week's takings.

So now here she was. Finally. Because every time she said she was on her way she got cold feet, insisting they were too busy for her to leave the café. She'd got away with her pathetic delaying tactics right up until this morning when Zoran had put his foot down and said all this shilly-shallying had to come to an end immediately or he'd have to go and talk to Bob himself.

'You want to do right by your aunt, don't you?' he'd demanded. 'And put these criminals behind bars before they do it again?'

Put like that, of course she did. Which was why she was here now, trying to ignore the fierce pulsing of her heart every time she relived that little scene. Zoran had looked so dark and brooding, like a man not to be trifled with. Masterful, that was the word — even in a white apron. That was some trick.

Bob was staring at her in a funny way.

'Are you deaf or something?' he said. 'I've asked you three times who it is you're after.'

Kerry roused herself, apologising profusely. She set about explaining how Bob could help, growing increasingly more uncomfortable as the story of how she'd been duped by a couple of con artists unfolded. This was the real reason she hadn't wanted to come along to the sandwich shop, of course. She felt exposed, stupid, a complete and utter idiot.

'And you fell for it, did you?'

'Yes, all right, Bob,' Kerry said, blushing furiously. 'But I'm not as stupid as all that. Because I recognised the man's voice.'

'Oh, aye?' Bob arched his brows.

'Cheese and pickle on white bread, no butter,' Kerry said triumphantly. 'Comes in the shop regularly. That's what he orders. Never varies. Either in what he asks for or the order of words he uses. Drives a white van. Overalls. Tattoos, bitten fingernails, an earring, shorn hair.'

'Just about describes every other person that walks through these doors,' he said.

'Come on, Bob, think! Like I said, he's a regular.'

'No. It's no use,' he said. 'I'd really love to help you, Kerry, but I just don't know how.'

Kerry sighed, her eyes roaming round the shop as if any minute now she expected the man who fitted her description to emerge from the ether. She'd been counting on Bob to pull out a name in five minutes. Then all it would take was a phone call to the police station and Cheese Sandwich Man plus accomplice would be behind bars before you could say salmonella. Her eyes alighted on the CCTV camera above the till.

'Eureka!'

Bob followed her gaze.

'No use asking to see that tape,' he said. 'There's no sound on it.'

'Doesn't matter,' Kerry said, exultant. 'Just keep it running as usual all week. When he comes in again and speaks his order — which I'm sure he will — make a note of the time, stop the tape and get in touch with me.'

Bob stroked his chin as if considering it.

'What is it he says again?'

Patiently she repeated the phrase. 'Cheese and pickle on white bread, no butter,' she said.

'Go on then,' Bob agreed. 'I might as well give it a go.'

★ ★ ★

Zoran was making something in a big, shiny bowl when Kerry arrived back, slipping in quietly through the kitchen door.

'You're in the doghouse with Alice,' he said, his eye leaving the bowl only for a second. 'Or you were till Dad dropped by. They're both out front making fans out of napkins.'

'Poor man,' Kerry said. 'She's got him right where she wants him now.'

The bowl was half full with a bright yellow mix, thick and glossy. She watched Zoran as carefully he dripped oil from a jug drop by drop, deftly whisking the contents of the bowl between each addition.

'What *is* that?' she asked him.

'Mayonnaise, of course. How did you get on? Any luck?'

'Why mayonnaise *of course?* It doesn't look anything like mayonnaise from where I'm standing. Anyway, mayonnaise comes in jars, doesn't it?'

Zoran rolled his eyes.

'Looks like Bob's going to help me unmask the conman. Or one half of the team, at least. After that it should be a doddle finding the other.'

'Good.'

'Can't you just tip that oil in all in one go?'

Zoran's performance was intriguing, without a doubt. But time was getting on and this mayonnaise was taking forever. If it was mayonnaise, that is. She still didn't necessarily believe him. Looked more like cake mix to her.

'Mayonnaise is an emulsion,' Zoran said. 'You have to add the oil drop by drop at first or else you'll break it. But now, see, I can add the rest in one go and it'll be fine.'

It was fascinating to watch how the whisk left trails of its own impression in the wobbly mixture. And to see that finally it had come to look like mayonnaise after all. But more golden and tempting than anything she'd seen in a jar.

'Wow, yes!' she exclaimed. 'Will you teach me how to do that? It would be so cool!'

He looked up at her, his eyes crinkling at the corners, grinning with pleasure at her sudden childlike expression of appreciation.

'Culinary magic, isn't it?' he said. 'And yes, of course I will.'

She grinned back and held his eyes. Her stomach gave a dip of pleasure and the air between them seemed to thicken with a sudden mutual yearning. Culinary magic wasn't the only kind of magic being performed right now, Kerry thought, holding her breath.

Then the spell was broken as Alice bustled in.

'I'm glad somebody's got time to stand around,' she said, her tone severe but her eyes soft. 'You don't need to bother with the napkins. It's all in hand.'

★   ★   ★

The rest of the afternoon was manic. Kerry had no time to dwell either on what had happened between Zoran and herself earlier — if, indeed, anything had happened — or on her exchange with Bob. All her focus was on getting everything right for tonight. Not even the smallest detail could be left to chance if the evening was going to be a success.

The most important thing was to keep her head. Not something that usually came easily to her, but, thanks to Alice's experience and Mehmet's new-found dogged devotion to her, coupled with Zoran's sure-handed approach to all things culinary, the only thing that could possibly let them down was a mix-up in bookings. And since she'd made herself responsible for that aspect of things, she thought she really ought to have a last-minute check.

Running her eyes down the page, she satisfied herself that everything was in order. Her parents were coming, and bringing Aunt Tazie, too, so for their sakes at least she hoped they'd put on a good show. She so wanted them to be proud of her efforts.

When she reached the last entry, her

heart began to race at the name she read there. *Mr and Mrs Brandon*, it said. And then a mobile number she recognised as easily as her own. Because she hadn't yet managed to bring herself to erase it from her own phone.

'Everything all right?'

Zoran was at her elbow.

'Who took this booking?' She spoke so sharply that Zoran, startled, backed away.

'Alice, I guess,' he said, peering at the writing. 'Or — well, maybe my dad did. Is something wrong?'

He looked at her, frowning slightly, anxious that somewhere along the line his dad had slipped up.

'No, It's fine,' she said.

Zoran seemed to be waiting for her to say more, but she dared not speak. She needed time to digest the fact that tonight Craig and his wife would be walking through the door of her restaurant and sitting down at a table to eat a meal right in front of her nose.

'I'll be getting on then.' Zoran's tone with her was as short as she realised her own with him must have been. He turned away, his manner brusque, and headed off towards the kitchen.

Oh, dear! Now she'd upset him, which she hadn't intended to at all. What was meant to be an adventure — their first night as a proper restaurant — was fast turning into a muddle.

Less than half an hour before they opened, Kerry's phone had bleeped. It was a picture message, from a number that she didn't recognise. A man, standing at the counter of what appeared to be Smiley's Sarnies, deep in conversation with Bob. Then her phone rang.

'Hi. It's Su-Lin Chen,' the voice said. 'From the sandwich shop. We spoke earlier.'

'Oh, hi! Did you send this picture just now? I guess you must have,' Kerry said.

'Evidence.' The girl spoke so quietly Kerry had trouble hearing her.

'But that's great,' she said. 'Have you got a name?'

There was a moment's silence on the other end of the phone before Su-Lin found her voice again.

'I'm afraid I've got something to tell

you that you might not want to hear,' she said, ignoring Kerry's question.

'Oh?'

'It's about Bob.'

Kerry was perplexed. What about Bob?

'Don't trust him. He's in on it!'

'What?' Kerry's heart started beating wildly.

'As soon as you left, he told me I had to stay in the back and make the food. He would serve the customers, he said. But I could see he was agitated. He kept trying to get someone on his phone but wouldn't leave a message. And then . . . ' She drew breath before rushing on. 'And then I saw him remove the videotape from the CCTV camera.'

Kerry gasped.

'I couldn't stop myself wondering why on earth he'd do something like that,' said Su-Lin. 'Unless he was trying to protect the guy who'd robbed you.'

She'd spent the rest of the day with her ears pricked, listening for any man who might come into the shop and say the words Kerry had repeated earlier, she said. She was in the back of the shop at the time, washing lettuce, but as soon as she heard that phrase, she'd grabbed her phone and snapped him.

'I could see Bob recognised the guy as soon as he came through the door,' she said. 'He did everything he could to stop the man saying those words. In case I overheard, I think. But even when he said *'Your usual, is it?'* it was like the guy was programmed or something. 'That's right, Bob, old mate,' he said. 'Cheese and pickle on white bread, no butter.' I could see Bob go pale. Then he leaned over the counter and mumbled something that made the other guy look worried, too. So then I knew for certain and took another snap.' After which, apparently, she'd nipped out the back and taken a picture of the man's number plate. The girl was a genius, without doubt, and Kerry told her as much.

'I've not had a minute before now to get back to you,' Su-Lin said, flushing with pleasure. 'Honestly, I've been worried sick. I almost rang the police myself but they'd know I shopped them, wouldn't they? I can't stop thinking Bob must have been able to read in my face that I know what he's been up to.'

'Oh, dear.' Kerry imagined this was more than likely. 'Where are you now?'

'Home,' the girl said. 'Biting my nails. Waiting for Bob's Mob to come round and sort me out.'

Diners had begun to arrive for the evening, smartly dressed and with an air of anticipation. She was meant to be at the door to greet them, but fortunately Mehmet, who'd swapped his casual clothes for the dandy vintage suit he'd worn the evening she'd first met him, had seen her on the phone and stepped into the breach. He really had turned out to be invaluable.

Briefly, Kerry explained that it was the restaurant launch. 'But leave this to me. Send me those other pics. I'll phone the police. That way Bob and his chums will be arrested before the evening's out and you won't need to worry about them any more,' she said.

'I hope so.' Su-Lin's voice quavered slightly.

Kerry decided she needed to get in

touch with the police immediately, if only to allay Sue-Lin's fears. Grabbing Mehmet, who was in the middle of taking an order, she told him to hold the fort just for five minutes.

'That's fine, my dear,' he said, as if he'd been waiting on in restaurants all his life. 'These lovely people are in excellent hands.'

The couple's smiling faces acted as a complete endorsement of his words, whereupon Kerry shot off to the tiny office she sometimes used. Ten minutes later, she emerged beaming triumphantly, having forwarded the photos to the police. It would be a matter of minutes, she was informed, and they'd have the owner of the van traced and the villains apprehended.

The small dining room had filled to bursting point in her absence with Mehmet and Alice dashing here, there and everywhere. Briefly, she wondered if she ought to give Zoran, the sole chef, a hand in the kitchen.

But just as she made a move in that direction, the sight of Craig and his wife, seated at a table for two in the middle of a room, stopped her in her tracks. She waited for that familiar stirring of longing and the ache of loss. But, oddly, all she felt instead was a huge feeling of release.

And in that moment she knew she'd finally floated free of the chains of love that had bound her to Craig. It would have been inappropriate to cheer, but grin she certainly could, as she sashayed over to his table, mistress of everything she surveyed. The look on his face, when he realised who it was asking him if he was enjoying his food, was one to be treasured. If he'd opted for the fish he'd have choked to death on a bone.

She kept up an inane prattle, hoping they liked the restaurant and that they'd come again, while deftly refilling their glasses. Mischievously, she was unable to restrain herself from remarking on his choice of the claret they'd brought with them.

'I'd have definitely said you were a claret man just from looking at you,' she teased, knowing full well that this was the wine he always chose whenever they ate out together.

It was a joy to watch his complexion turn the same colour as the wine in his glass.

'You all right, darling?' his wife asked, looking worried for a moment.

'I'm fine,' Craig muttered, staring at his plate. 'Something went down the wrong way, that's all.'

Kerry danced off to the next table, greeting diners, waving at her mum and dad and Aunt Tazie, who looked in rude health, considering the operation she'd not long since endured. The room was full of contented diners and the evening had turned into a huge success.

And when Sue-Lin appeared at the door, saw the tables that hadn't been cleared, and set about doing something about it, it got even better. She couldn't go back to the sandwich shop in the morning, she said. So she'd come here to ask for a job.

'As from tonight you join the team,' Kerry said.

'Waitress in a proper restaurant,' Sue-Lin sighed. 'My dream come true.'

* * *

And now Kerry and Zoran were alone in the kitchen sharing a bottle of wine at the table. Everyone had left. The nice police officer who'd called with the good news that the culprits were finally in custody, who'd stayed for dessert, was the first to go. Then Sue-Lin had hopped on her bike, promising she'd be back at ten the next day. Finally, Alice departed, after saying what fun it had been and dropping the bombshell that now she was sure Kerry could cope alone, especially as she had a new pair of hands with Su-Lin, she really did think it was time to retire.

She had a new interest in her life now, she said, with a sidelong look at Mehmet, who took her arm proprietarily as he led her away.

'But any time you need a hand, please call me,' he said, over his shoulder. 'It's given me a new lease of life, working here.'

'OK,' said Kerry, 'what about showing me how to make mayonnaise, now we're finally alone?'

Zoran's eyes gleamed over his glass. 'You serious?' he said. 'It's nearly midnight.'

But already Kerry had darted to the fridge to get eggs, and was now opening cupboard doors and drawers in order to assemble everything else they'd need. She felt wired, brimming with so much adrenalin after the events of the night that the idea of going to bed was ludicrous.

Zoran took her through it step by step, cracking the egg, skilfully separating the yolk from the white, then sliding it into a bowl.

'How did you do that?' Kerry asked, amazed.

'Practice,' Zoran said. 'Now, a couple of drops of vinegar, mustard and seasoning.'

Next, he handed her the whisk.

'Me?' she squeaked. 'What do I do?'

'Whisk it all together.'

Well, that bit was easy enough anyway!

'Now for the hard part. You must add the oil, drop by drop, remember. And keep whisking.'

Just in time he stopped her from tipping in too much oil, by staying her wrist with his hand.

'Look,' he said, 'if I stand here behind you and take the whisk too, it'll remind you not to pour it all in at once.'

So, drop by drop, Zoran's hand lightly on her own, Kerry continued.

'Don't forget — keep whisking.' His breath touched her neck softly, sending her into a trance.

'Oh, it's starting to look like mayonnaise at last,' she said.

She felt Zoran's lips brush the hollow of her neck, where it joined her collarbone, and shivered deliciously.

'How am I doing?'

Gently, but determinedly, Zoran removed the whisk from Kerry's hand. She put up no resistance, but simply slid round to face him. She longed to relax into his embrace, but first there was something she needed to say.

'I'm sorry if I was rude earlier,' she said. 'By the reservation book. It was just, well, an ex of mine had been booked in. And his wife.'

'Oh?' Zoran hardly seemed to be listening. His arms were round her waist and he drew her closer. 'An ex, did you say?'

She nodded.

Zoran sighed. 'Kerry,' he said. 'The past — it can stifle you. Look what it did to my dad. But look at him now. He's happy. Moving forwards. We all have pasts. The trick is to know when to relinquish it and start living in the present.'

'Wise words,' she said softly.

She leaned in closer for Zoran's kiss, certain that for the two of them that sweet moment had just arrived.

# CURTAIN UP

# 1

Chrissie had concluded that it would have been easier to corral a team of revelling rugby players on to the minibus than the nine thirteen-year-olds she'd be chaperoning for the next six weeks. What with the squealing and the pushing and shoving about who sat next to whom, plus the incessant banging on from that Kirsty girl about needing the window seat, Chrissie's temples were already beginning to throb.

The parents were even worse. Mums, in her opinion, should be stoical when saying goodbye to their offspring. A cheery smile, a bright wave, a firm reminder about hygiene and homework were more than sufficient, to her way of thinking. But, in at least two cases, she'd ended up literally prising tearful mothers away from their daughters with dire warnings about the traffic they'd hit if they ran any later, before firmly ejecting them from the bus by the seats of their skinny designer jeans.

Anyone would think the little actresses were being shunted off to some Dickensian boarding school, not off on tour in a professional company, giving *A Musical Midsummer Night's Dream* to adoring audiences in six towns in as many weeks.

The girls had volunteered for this gig — clamoured even, running the gauntlet of the audition process like hard-bitten old pros. Their mums should be glad their girls had made the grade. Now they could all go home and start bragging to the neighbours.

It was a relief when Chrissie finally managed to squeeze the last parent through the ever-narrowing gap in the sliding door out on to the street beyond. At last they were off and Chrissie could sit down.

She fell into the only seat left. Eddie Dawlish looked up from his newspaper and smiled shyly. 'What a piece of luck to have adult male company all the way to Nottingham,' had been her first thought when Wesley Jenkins, the tour manager, rang her to say there'd be one more on board. Her second thought was that he might be fat, bald and smelly. Such men did exist, even in the theatre.

'His car's packed up and he needs to get to the theatre before the rest of the crew,' Wesley had told her.

'Why?'

'Because that's what Eddie does,' he said, implying it was none of her business.

Chrissie hadn't liked his tone. She wasn't some menial to be dumped on just because it was convenient for other people. She reminded Wesley she was *in loco parentis.* What would the girls' parents think about some strange man stuck in a confined space with their precious cargo all the way to Nottingham?

'Has he got clearance?' she demanded.

'Chrissie. He's just a bloke who wants a lift, that's all,' Wesley spluttered. 'Just say yes.'

It may have been a while since she'd last appeared on stage, but Chrissie hadn't forgotten all she'd learned. She delivered an eight-second pause that reminded Wesley exactly who held the power in this transaction.

In the end she'd agreed. But he had to promise to sit next to her and to keep right away from the girls. He might be the best lighting engineer in the business, but you could never be too sure.

Thirty minutes into their journey, Chrissie had decided that her travelling companion was a man of few words. It wasn't as if she hadn't given Eddie Dawlish enough opportunities to speak. But when every pause she left simply remained dangling between them, she felt obliged to keep talking. Silence, to Chrissie, was like a gaping wound. She just hoped he didn't think she was coming across as all me, me, me.

She'd imagined it would be impossible to go wrong by asking him what lighting engineering actually entailed. But his reply was brief. He obviously thought his job wasn't particularly worth enlarging on, and seemed much more interested in hers.

It was rather refreshing to meet someone so lacking in self-obsession.

Eddie was like a big old teddy bear. Solid, affable, giving the impression he'd put up with anything without complaint. Not even the raucous shrieking from the girls at the back of the bus made him flinch, Chrissie observed, slipping a painkiller under her tongue while mentally reciting the names of her new charges to check she'd got them right.

Kirsty was the one that stood out, of course, with her complaining. Then there was Lorna, who looked petrified, twins Ariella and Trilby — would she ever tell them apart and had their mum chosen those names for a joke? Blonde and buxom Chelsea, tall and Titian-haired Tanya, and finally Millie, Ruby and Jess, who all seemed to be getting on like a house on fire, thank goodness.

She cast a discreet eye over Eddie's appearance. Casually dressed, though not in the actorly sense, where even the socks went through a rigorous vetting procedure. Just jeans and a bashed-up leather jacket.

'So, how did you get into chaperoning kids?' he asked. 'You don't really look the mothering sort.'

Chrissie assumed he was alluding to her height — or rather lack of it — and her rather boyish figure. 'An Audrey Hepburn type' was the phrase her agent had used to describe her, back in the days when she'd had an agent.

'Believe me, I'm not,' she said self-deprecatingly. 'A friend of mine was sick, so I volunteered to step in at the last minute. Thought it would make a change from bar work, which is what I used to do when I was 'resting'.'

She sketched imaginary quotation marks round the word so often employed by actors as a synonym for 'out of work'. Eddie nodded sympathetically.

He knew all about the life, he said. Lurching from one job to another, no pension, nothing in the bank for a rainy day. Speaking for himself, he had nothing lined up after this job, which was a real worry, especially with a bill for God knows how much from the garage for fixing his car. Chrissie commiserated.

'I sort of drifted into chaperoning full-time in the end for that same reason,' she said. 'In your job I bet experience counts, though, which must bring in work eventually. But in mine it's the opposite. You can soon get too old in this profession.'

Aware she might be coming across as self-pitying — not to mention ancient — she quickly perked up again.

'I've managed to keep my hand in over the years, though. Chorus, the odd pantomime. So I'm not complaining.'

'I suppose if the theatre is in your blood you can't bear to be away for too long.'

'Eddie, that's exactly the right phrase. In the blood. You've summed me up perfectly,' she exclaimed. 'Even now, I get butterflies before curtain up, still swoon at the sniff of a stick of greasepaint, still whip out my autograph book the moment the leading man walks by. Thinking about it, that must be why I took to chaperoning right away, because deep down I'm still a child myself.'

Eddie glanced towards the window and the damp, grey, traffic-filled streets they were leaving behind. Was this a hint that he wanted her to shut up? She'd always longed to be the enigmatic type, yet the art of discretion had always eluded her. At this rate there'd be nothing he didn't know about her by the time they reached Nottingham.

If it hadn't been for that dreadful Kirsty Granger playing up again, she'd probably have gone even further and launched into that stupid fantasy of hers, boring him even further to death. The one where some big-shot producer — Andrew Lloyd Webber, say — walks past the open dressing-room door where she's killing time by belting out the big number. Which so impresses the big-shot producer that, before you can say, 'You're fired, she's hired', the leading lady is booted back into the chorus line and Chrissie has taken her place.

Fortunately, Kirsty, complaining about the air-conditioning this time, saved her from herself in the nick of time. A right little prima donna, that one. Chrissie had heard her complaining to her mum earlier about how ridiculous it was that she had to share her role of Puck with two other girls.

'What do we need them for? I've seen them act, and they're both rubbish.'

'You know the law, Kirsty. You're minors. You can only work so many hours a week and that includes rehearsals and waiting around.' Mrs Granger had explained this patiently and quietly, but her voice turned steely as she added, 'But when you're older you'll have the big roles all to yourself. Just keep up your dancing practice every day and lay off the pizzas.'

Such words of wisdom!

Another squeal had Chrissie up and out of her seat in a flash. There was nothing for it but to sort this girl out before the others took it on themselves. And from the mutinous expressions on their faces, her intervention came not a moment too soon.

On reaching Nottingham, they dropped Eddie off at the theatre and drove on towards their lodgings, where it quickly became worryingly apparent that the group atmosphere had disintegrated still further. Chrissie had gone off to butter up the landlady, briefly leaving the girls to sort out the sleeping arrangements between themselves. Heading back to her room, the sound of raised voices made her quicken her steps to the first floor landing, where their four rooms were situated.

'I need the bed by the window and I need more space in the wardrobe because I've brought more clothes.'

Kirsty stood in the middle of the room, daring the other girls to challenge her.

'But Lorna doesn't want to share with you.' Ariella, the feistier twin, who'd shouted down Kirsty on the bus, was having none of it. With both hands she tugged Kirsty's case down from the bed and set it down heavily, just missing Kirsty's toes. Kirsty kept her ground, unnerved.

'No one wants to share with you,' Trilby joined in.

There were mutters of agreement from the others, even from Lorna, who was hiding behind Trilby.

'Come on, girls,' Chrissie pleaded. 'Do the maths. There are three bedrooms with three beds each and nine of you.'

Kirsty looked up at the ceiling, indicating boredom with a flicker of her eyes. Eight other pairs of eyes remained fixed on Chrissie. There was no way she could beat this lot on her own.

'We have to be a threesome,' Ruby said, grabbing Millie and Jess by the arm.

'And the twins can't be separated,' Tanya said, 'and I can't be separated from them.'

'Anyway, Lorna needs the window more than her because she's claustrophobic.' Chelsea glared at Kirsty. 'And she needs me, too, because she's scared of *her*. And I'm not sharing a room with anyone who calls me fat.'

'We'll discuss this properly tomorrow,' Chrissie sighed. 'Meanwhile, Kirsty, you can share with me. My room has two beds.'

'Didn't want to share with a bunch of kids, anyway.' Kirsty grabbed her case, deliberately bumping it against Chelsea's legs, then muttering an insincere sorry as she followed Chrissie from the room. Chrissie decided to ignore Chelsea's muttered response of 'Loser' aimed, she sincerely hoped, not at herself but at Kirsty.

'Don't you think you should try to act a little more tolerantly of the other girls?' Chrissie said as, back in her own room, Kirsty rummaged in her case.

Kirsty shrugged. 'Whatever,' she said, and trotted off to the bathroom, clutching her pink fluorescent washbag.

Chrissie sighed. At this rate, the next six weeks were going to be a long haul. After an age spent thumping her lumpy pillow, prowling around her mattress in search of the one spot where she wouldn't come under attack from vicious bed-springs, she finally drifted off to sleep.

But, actually, as the first week of their tour drew to a close, Chrissie couldn't believe how fast the time was spinning by. Soon they'd be moving on to Manchester. She'd been so busy that she'd barely had time to draw breath.

Not content with looking after her own charges — which for the most part entailed searching for lost combs, lost lip gloss and, in one case, a rather beautiful charm bracelet of Lorna's that she'd turned both bedroom and dressing-room over to look for, without success — Chrissie often volunteered her services wherever else they were needed.

She made camomile tea for Titania and gave Indian head massages to the Mechanics. She sprayed Bottom with spring water to cool his burning cheeks after so long trapped beneath his ass's head, and trotted to the bar at regular intervals for gin and tonic for Oberon, smiling sweetly as she reminded them to put it on his slate. If asked, she would even have swept the stage just so she could feel truly in the thick of it.

★   ★   ★

'You learn something new all the time in this job.' She was in the dressing-room shared by the two actresses who played Helena and Hermia, the two young humans bewitched by Oberon's love potion.

Helena — Chrissie always forgot to call the actress by her less glamorous given name of Maggie — had been attempting to untangle the knots from her wig.

Somewhere in her bag she had a detangling comb — the proper tool for the job — and now she was busy searching for it.

'Oberon's been explaining the betting system to me. I'm to place a bet on Greaselightning in the 3.15 at Haydock,' Chrissie said proudly.

Helena looked up from her bag. The dressing-table was cluttered with all the make-up, old receipts and sweet wrappers she'd come across while looking for the thing she really wanted.

'Make sure you get the money off him first. He has a short memory, that one,' she said, withdrawing a thick bundle of what Chrissie immediately realised could only be twenty-pound notes and carelessly adding them to the pile.

'My boob-job money,' she added, noticing Chrissie's jaw drop. 'I know I should put it in the bank, but, honestly, it's probably safer in my bag than lining the pockets of some dodgy bank manager.'

'There's a safe in my digs,' Chrissie said. 'Surely there's one in yours?'

'You haven't seen my landlord. Wouldn't trust him as far as I could throw him. No thanks, it's staying where it is.'

Chrissie banged on for a while about banks still being the safest place to keep your money, even going so far as to volunteer to go with Maggie to the nearest branch of her own bank as soon as they got the opportunity and help her set up an account, but still Maggie was having none of it. For a woman in her mid-twenties, she seemed extraordinarily impractical. So she changed the subject to Maggie's boobs.

'Why on earth do you want to be a D cup, Maggie?' she asked.

'I'm typecast, Chrissie,' Maggie said. 'How d'you think I got the role of Helena? Painted maypole, Hermia calls her. There's not much call for maypoles in Hollywood, painted or otherwise.'

'Well, I think you're mad,' Chrissie said. 'About getting your boobs done and about wanting to go to Hollywood. Not to mention refusing to put your money in a bank.'

'Chrissie, take a chill pill, will you, sweetheart.'

'But I'm worried for you. Carrying all those notes around. You might get mugged. This is not your home patch, you know. You don't know where's safe and where's not.'

In the end, Maggie capitulated.

'What are you doing?'

Maggie was holding out her bundle of notes. 'What's it look like? I'm giving it to you. So you can put it in your landlady's safe.'

'Oh, no,' Chrissie said. 'Please don't ask me to be responsible for your money. There must be hundreds in there.'

'One thousand five hundred, actually. Nearly a boob's worth.'

Chrissie gasped at the sum.

'It'd only be for a night,' Maggie said. 'Two at most. Look, it was your idea.'

Chrissie thought it over. She had another three hours max at the theatre before returning to her digs. Then the cash would go straight in the safe.

'Oh, go on then,' she sighed, wondering when she was going to learn to mind her own business.

But, in the end, it was too late to do

anything about putting the money in the safe. By the time they got back that night, the landlady had gone to bed and the next morning, when it was time to leave for the theatre again, she was nowhere to be found.

There was no alternative but to keep hold of the cash.

If there was a bank not too far away from where they were playing, then maybe she could persuade Helena — Maggie — to pop out and open an account before the matinée began. She'd even go with her if she wanted. She got the distinct impression that, while Shakespeare presented the actress with no challenge, form-filling was an entirely different kettle of fish.

Best thing all round, of course, would be to give the bundle straight back to Maggie and sort out a mutually convenient time for them both to pop out and find a bank. Almost as if she'd heard her summons, Maggie popped her head round the door.

'Thank God you're here, Chrissie,' she said. Even dressed in leg warmers and wired up to her iPod, Maggie still managed to look glamorously sylph-like. A bit dotty, but sylph-like nonetheless.

'Titania's throwing a wobbly,' Maggie said. 'She can't find her lucky charm and she says she won't do the matinée without it. We've looked everywhere and none of us can find it.'

Titania's lucky charm was a carved wooden elephant that could be held in the palm of one hand. It was the third time this week something of hers had gone missing, and Chrissie was beginning to think she was just attention seeking. It couldn't be easy acting opposite Anthony Brice's Oberon and being upstaged every night by a national treasure.

'I'm right on it,' she said, heading for the door. 'When I get back we need to have a talk about your boob money, remember,' she called out over her shoulder. 'But for now, just keep an eye on my bag, will you?'

Maggie beamed at her and gave her the thumbs up.

'Honestly,' Chrissie thought, 'that girl really shouldn't be let out on her own.'

In the end, Titania did do the matinée, even though her elephant had failed to turn up. Her performance was more lacklustre than usual; Chrissie felt responsible as she'd promised Titania she'd find the charm and in the end she'd failed, despite turning the place upside down.

When she'd offered to do a head massage for her to make up for it, Titania had refused rather sharply, saying it would take more than a head massage to make up for her loss, and now she wasn't speaking to her.

It had been a rotten day all told. Oberon had forgotten all about the tenner he owed her, just as Maggie had predicted, and one of the twins, Trilby, who was playing Mustardseed today and who had to fly, had fallen and scraped her knee, blaming Kirsty for blocking her landing, which Kirsty had naturally denied.

In her sister's defence, Ariella had accused Kirsty of being jealous because her applause hadn't been as loud as Trilby's had been. Kirsty had responded by saying that the only reason the audience had applauded Trilby was because she'd been showing her knickers, at which point Trilby fell on Kirsty and a catfight had ensued.

Now both girls were in disgrace and were due to be disciplined the following morning before they boarded the coach to Manchester. And from the look the producer shot Chrissie as he marched off, she was certain she was in for a ticking off, too, for her inability to keep order.

On top of everything, she had to oversee the packing. If only she could leave them to it, but with tensions running as high as they were, unless she stood over them it would only be a matter of time before someone took it upon herself to throw Kirsty's suitcase out of the window. The way she felt right now, that person might very well be herself.

At least she'd have the pleasure of Eddie's company again tomorrow, on the road. Instigated by him and not by herself, either.

'Of course you can travel with us again,' she'd told him, when she found him hovering outside the girls' dressing-room just before the fight exploded. 'I look forward to resuming our conversation.'

'Me, too,' he'd said, looking bashful. Pleased, though. He definitely looked pleased.

Chrissie suppressed a yawn. If she sat any longer on her bed, she'd fall asleep, she decided, and heaved herself up. Then she remembered Maggie and her wretched money. In all the hoop-la with Titania's lucky charm and the even bigger hoop-la that followed with the girls, not to mention the energy she'd used up trying to work out how best to remind Oberon about the tenner he owed her without hurting his feelings, she'd forgotten all about persuading Maggie to take her money back.

At least she could make sure it got put in the safe for their one remaining night in Nottingham. Mrs Penny, the landlady, was definitely in — she'd just heard her telling off one of the girls for running up and down the stairs.

No doubt something else Chrissie would be held personally responsible for. She sighed, reaching for her bag. A woman with a cluttered bag was a woman with a cluttered mind, she'd read once. Well, that was her all right. Best thing would be to tip everything out on to the bed, she decided, when she'd scrabbled about in vain for long enough.

She must have been staring at the contents spilled out on to the bed for a full five minutes before finally concluding that this was a problem that was not going to go away. Maggie's precious bundle of twenty-pound notes simply wasn't there and no amount of plea-bargaining with God was going to magic it back.

# 2

Chrissie had made a pillow out of her sweater to rest her head on for the journey to their next stop, Manchester. If only sleep would come and blot everything out, so that when next she opened her eyes and looked in her bag, Maggie's bundle of notes would miraculously have been returned, as clean and new as the first time she'd seen them.

But she was far too agitated to settle. Sooner or later she was going to have to face Maggie and own up. Fifteen hundred pounds. Nearly a boob's worth, she remembered Maggie saying, her perfect smile lighting up her face.

Why on earth did the girl have to flash her savings at her in the first place? And why had she, Chrissie, agreed to Maggie's daft idea of asking Mrs Penny, her landlady, to put it in her safe overnight? No use blaming Maggie, though. All of this could have been avoided if only she'd learned to mind her own business for once in her life.

While she was punching her makeshift cushion so she could re-position it in a more comfortable spot, Eddie, the lighting engineer, sat down next to her.

'Catching up on your beauty sleep?'

'Eddie! I forgot about you.' A wan smile was all she could muster in her fragile state.

'Story of my life,' he joked.

On any other occasion she'd have leapt at the opportunity to chat, but right now conversation was the last thing she wanted to engage in. It appeared that Eddie, on the other hand, had got a sudden taste for it. Last time he'd sat next to her on the bus she'd barely managed to wring more than a dozen words out of him. This time nothing would shut him up.

He held forth on everything, from the inferiority of the breakfasts he'd had to put up with while in Nottingham and his fervent wishes that Manchester might provide him with better lodgings, to his ruminations on the route they were taking, which wouldn't have been his choice. In the end, good manners forced her to abandon her elusive attempts at unconsciousness. There was nothing for it but to sit up and look interested.

Which, actually, she couldn't help being in the end. Eddie had a dry wit and his stories were always funny. Every time he made her smile she was almost able to forget about the mire she was now up to her neck in.

'The girls are quiet,' he observed, glancing round the bus. Turning back to Chrissie, he added, 'Thank heavens for small mercies, eh?'

'You haven't heard then?'

'Obviously not. What have I missed? Been caught smuggling male groupies into their rooms, have they? Or running a poker den after lights out?'

'Worse. Fighting. Well, scrapping really. But in front of the Boss.'

'Will Granger? The producer? The man who makes Alan Sugar look like the Good Fairy?'

'And Brian Sewell sound like a barrow boy.'

Eddie's crumpled brow registered that although he was well aware who the former icon was, he'd never heard of the latter.

'The art critic. You must have heard him on the radio. Consonants so sharp you could slice through granite with them. Vowels so pure they make your ears ring.'

'Oh, him. He's scary.'

Chrissie nodded.

Eddie chewed over the information Chrissie had just fed him. 'Fighting, eh?' he said. 'I'm impressed.'

'Granger wasn't. Said any more of it and they'd be out on their ears, and showed them a file of all the other wannabe Mustardseeds and Pucks. Thing is, I'm just as mortified as them. After he'd let them go he kept me behind and gave me an even bigger dressing down.'

'Oh, dear. I'm sorry.'

Chrissie was grateful for the sympathy.

'What did he say?'

'Oh, you know. What you'd expect. That as chaperone I was expected to blah-blah-blah and that if I thought I wasn't up to it maybe I should blah-blah-blah or perhaps I should, y'know . . . '

'Yadder, yadder, yadder,' Eddie said, filling in the rest of it. 'You don't really want to talk about it.'

'Exactly.'

She could have said that, added to her woes, fifteen hundred quid had disappeared from her handbag while she was supposed to be looking after it. But there were some things you didn't broadcast.

Chrissie was suddenly overwhelmed with exhaustion. What with one thing and another, she'd barely had a wink of sleep the previous night. A situation that had been made worse by Kirsty snoring away merrily as only someone with a clear conscience can do. The brat!

'If you don't mind, Eddie,' she said, 'I could do with a bit of a kip.'

'Oh, 'course. Right. Yeah. Sure, go ahead. I'll — er — read my magazine then.'

Eddie made a big show of retrieving a copy of *What Car?* from his scruffy leather manbag and, with a great deal of unnecessary fuss, finally settled down to read it.

Chrissie closed her eyes and resumed praying. Her makeshift cushion gradually slipped from beneath her head, leaving her lolling against the cold, unforgiving surface of the minibus window. She sighed as one more hole in the road gave her poor, addled brain yet another jolt.

★　★　★

Maybe she should have knocked before bursting in on Kirsty that same night. But she hadn't imagined she'd be in bed with the light off at the relatively early time of nine o'clock. The muffled sobs that greeted her as she crept into the room pulled Chrissie up short, totally distracting her from her own dilemma of how much longer she could run around avoiding Maggie and making excuses as to when they could fix a time to go to the bank, to deposit her 'boob job' cash.

In a flash she was kneeling beside Kirsty's bed, coaxing her from beneath the bedclothes, with a tissue.

'I'm not good enough,' Kirsty blubbed into her tissue. 'And I'll never be good enough for them.'

'What? Not good enough? Good enough for who? Tell me.'

Chrissie braced herself for some sort of acknowledgement that her behaviour so far had been out of order. She was taken aback at what came next. Did Kirsty really not care how much the other girls — who'd been giving her an even wider berth than usual since their telling off — disliked her?

'My dad hasn't been to see me once,' she sobbed.

'But your mum has,' Chrissie reminded her, like the poor kid needed reminding.

It had been a flying visit, to watch Kirsty's performance back in Nottingham. Afterwards, Mrs Granger had presented her with a list of notes. Nothing major, was her way of expressing it. Just a few suggestions about how Kirsty could improve.

Chrissie would have expressed it differently. More like crippling blows to the confidence that would have made any young girl less determined to succeed than Kirsty give up acting altogether and take up a less demanding pastime. Half an hour later, she'd left. She had an appointment, so she said.

'It's 'cos of me they're getting a divorce,' Kirsty sobbed.

Chrissie hadn't known anything about Kirsty's parents separating. She felt bitter towards Mrs Granger. If only she'd let her know there was trouble at home, she would have tried to be more understanding of the girl. And made an effort to get the other girls to try to be a bit more tolerant of her prima donna behaviour.

Perched on Kirsty's bed, she felt bad that once again she'd allowed the others to pair off instead of insisting they take turns to share a room with Kirsty. Now it must seem to everyone, none more than Kirsty herself, that Chrissie — who was meant to have her interests at heart — was condoning the cold shoulder treatment that the girls had taken to a whole new level since arriving in Manchester.

Could their behaviour be seen as bullying? If so, then Chrissie, as the adult, was definitely to blame for letting things get out of hand. Yet if anyone was doing the bullying, it was surely Kirsty. She seemed to derive huge delight from littering the other girls' paths with insults, and Chrissie had lost count of the number of times she'd mopped up tears brought on by one of Kirsty's snide comments.

'It's the same row over and over.' Kirsty stumbled over her words. 'Dad says Mum spends too much time driving me here, there and everywhere for auditions, and too much money on classes and clothes. He says she's obsessed. She says *he's* obsessed with his job. Then he says he's got no choice if she keeps giving him bills all the time.'

Chrissie did her best to reassure Kirsty that her parents loved her very much. It was all she could do and she hoped it was true. She was no psychologist, but it struck her that Kirsty was so full of self-loathing right now that she didn't think she was worthy of love and friendship from any quarter.

Hence her dogged determination to make damn sure that she rejected the friendship of others well before they rejected any overtures from her. Add to this the latest lambasting from the producer and it was no surprise the poor girl was falling apart. Chrissie had a lot of work to do if she wanted to fix this.

'Come with us to see *Marley And Me* tomorrow,' she said, stroking Kirsty's hair. 'It's a day off, remember. We can sit and eat chocolate while we watch.'

Kirsty screwed up her face. 'Mum says chocolate's just brown lard,' she said.

'Does she now?'

Kirsty's mother had a lot to answer for, in her opinion. And her dad too. Poor kid, playing piggy in the middle while those two slugged it out over her head.

'It's late now, Kirsty. Do you think you can go to sleep?'

Kirsty nodded. Her eyes were already closing.

'Thanks a lot for listening, Chrissie,' she said, squeezing her hand feebly.

Chrissie squeezed back, more firmly. 'That's what I'm here for,' she said, wishing that the lump in her throat would dissolve.

* ★ ★

Chrissie had been so mortified by the scene in the producer's office that she'd taken to watching out for him so she could avoid any more of his disdainful glares. Now she was dodging two people. Luckily, this being a theatre, there were always lots of props to hide behind. Or inside. Laying her hands on an ass's head would be a doddle if she got desperate.

She'd taken up permanent residence in the wings during rehearsals. If there was to be any more sparring among her girls, she wanted to be first at the scene to break it up. The location also offered the added advantage of an excellent view of the actors in rehearsal, which was always a pleasure.

It was from this position that the fruitily imperious tones of the actor playing Oberon reached her ears as he crept up behind her in slippered feet to take his cue.

'Chrissie, my dear sweet girl, you couldn't do a chap an immense favour, I don't suppose?'

Chrissie jumped. Among other things, *A Midsummer Night's Dream* was a play about magic. Fearing she was about to be tapped for another loan, Chrissie prayed for a spell that could render her invisible.

'Now, don't look at me like that, dear girl,' Sir Anthony said. 'I'm not going to ask you for money.'

Chrissie tried not to look too relieved.

'Thing is, I've had a tip-off on the 4.45 at Kempton Park,' he said. 'A dead cert. Such a certainty, in fact, that nothing less than a bet of one hundred pounds will suffice.'

'Oh?'

'Unfortunately, the dead cert's name has gone clean out of my geriatric head.'

'Well, it's not the only thing,' Chrissie almost said. 'There's a small matter of a tenner, too.' Unfortunately, Sir Anthony, though blessed with a huge talent, wasn't similarly blessed with telepathy. If she wanted her money back, she was going to have to ask for it, which would be a breach in protocol on a par with giving the Queen a pat on the backside.

'On my dressing table, back page of the

*Mail*, red circle round it,' he said. 'Funny how I can remember circling it but can't remember its bally name.'

'Let me pop back and get it for you,' Chrissie said. 'You're on in a couple of minutes.'

'Such a kind girl,' he called after her, as if she'd volunteered for the task. 'And don't worry about your tenner. I've had a big win this weekend — made some serious money. So you'll definitely get it back.'

Though delighted he'd remembered, Chrissie wasn't about to hold her breath.

The newspaper was there, where he'd said it would be, on his dressing room table. She could have just picked it up and returned the way she'd come. But something was niggling her.

Sir Anthony's inability to pick a winner was a standing joke among the entire company. And when he wasn't losing money on the gee-gees, he was paying out every penny he earned to a succession of ex-wives.

Chrissie racked her brain. What if Sir Anthony had acquired the pot of gold he was claiming to be in possession of, by foul means? Desperation can turn even honest men into thieves. Of course, he would have had to have the opportunity first.

Yesterday, Chrissie had gone haring off to search for Titania's missing lucky charm, leaving Maggie in the girls' dressing room in sole attendance. But there was no saying who might have popped in to pass the time of day while she'd been gone.

Maggie was the sociable type. She liked to catch up on gossip. How many times had Chrissie herself been invited to keep her company between acts? It was keeping Maggie company that had got Chrissie into this fix in the first place.

She hated herself for doing what she was about to do. This was a peer of the realm she was suspecting. Knighted by the Queen, no less! But she had to put her mind at rest. It was a relief when none of the drawers in Sir Anthony's dressing table would give, no matter how hard she tugged. If he had stolen her money — correction, Maggie's money — she didn't think she could bear to discover it.

Chrissie moved on from tugging at drawers that wouldn't open to picking up all the clothes, towels and magazines tossed carelessly on to the floor, checking that no bundle of notes had been stashed in them, before adding them to the neat pile she was making.

Among them was the midnight-blue waistcoat, lined in red silk, that she'd seen Sir Anthony wearing on a couple of occasions. When she'd remarked on how stylish he looked in it, he'd said that it had once belonged to Larry Olivier, who'd been generous enough to lend it to him when he'd been a struggling young actor, adding that he'd hung on to it for so long that the opportunity to return it came and went, which was why it was still in his possession.

Of course, it could have been a whopping great fib, but all the same . . . Unable to stop herself, Chrissie stroked the waistcoat lovingly, then held it to her nose and sniffed it, in case a trace of the great Olivier remained.

'What a tender picture!'

She only half-recognised the woman leaning in the doorway. Leonie, she thought her name was. Or maybe it was Lydia? Titania's understudy, anyway.

'There's life in the old dog yet, then.' A slow smile of glee spread over her thin face. 'Don't worry. Your secret's safe with me!'

What on earth was she getting at? Surely not that Chrissie had a thing for Sir Anthony? The man was old enough to be her grandfather, practically. Then she remembered that his last squeeze had been at least five years younger than herself.

'Don't be ridiculous,' she snapped. 'You can't possibly think there's anything going on between me and Sir Anthony.'

Grabbing the copy of the *Daily Mail* she'd been sent to retrieve, Chrissie bulldozed her way past.

'Methinks the lady doth protest too much,' came the echo.

'Wrong play, mutt-head,' Chrissie muttered, turning the corner. 'Ouch! Watch where you're going!'

She was almost felled by Kirsty,

hurtling towards her like an out-of-control boulder. Chrissie had never seen her so animated offstage; her face shone with pure delight. Peering into the distance behind her, it soon became apparent why.

'I promise to bring her back in time for her matinée tomorrow,' the flash-looking stranger drawled. Then, with a glance at his expensive-looking watch, he added, 'Just tell me what time.'

Kirsty's father! Teeth too white, skin too tanned, cologne far too overpowering. In a moment, she summed him up. A man who obviously invested in the outer show at the expense of — what? Kirsty? Well, he was here now, so better late than never.

Except he couldn't just turn up out of the blue like this and haul Kirsty away. Chrissie didn't enjoy being a party pooper, not with Kirsty clinging on to her daddy while she gazed up at him so adoringly. But she'd had her orders. After what Kirsty had told her about her parents splitting up, she'd checked the girl's file to see if she'd missed something.

And it seemed she had.

Under 'responsible adult' was written *Mandi Granger*. There was no mention of a Mr Granger. As far as the law saw it, that meant the only person with the authority to turn up at the stage door and whisk Kirsty away was her mother.

Chrissie explained all this to both of them, albeit in a somewhat roundabout way. She'd grown to know Kirsty quite well over the last couple of weeks and had a pretty good idea about which way this could go. She was soon proved right.

'But he's my dad!' Kirsty squawked. 'And if you don't let me go, I'll . . . I'll . . . '

She looked around for something to kick. Finding nothing, she flung herself on to the ground and began to weep. She was very good, Chrissie couldn't deny it.

Mr Granger — 'call me Nat' — used more subtle tactics. He was obviously distressed at the sight of his daughter battering all hell out of the floor with her heels and those tiny fists. Couldn't she see how much Kirsty wanted this, he pleaded, appealing to her humanity. And how dreadful it would be to deny her this treat?

Chrissie couldn't help but sympathise. All the other girls, bar Kirsty, had been whisked off by various relatives and friends of relatives over the weekend and it hardly seemed fair that Kirsty was forced to stay behind.

But she had her orders. Nat Granger's name wasn't in the file, therefore Nat Granger couldn't take Kirsty away. Not for an hour and most definitely not overnight.

'I wouldn't have put you down as a jobsworth, Miss Whatever-your-name-is,' he said bitterly.

Chrissie gulped. Is that how she sounded? A quick replay of her words and the answer came back immediately. Yes. A jobsworth of the worst kind. She was suddenly filled with self-loathing.

'I don't suppose it can do any harm,' she said, after searching her soul and discovering that being a human being was far more important to her than being Kirsty's minder.

Within seconds, Kirsty had picked

herself up off the floor, all trace of tears gone.

'We just need to settle on the ground rules first,' Chrissie added.

* * *

It had been worth a try. In her head she and Eddie were already having dinner in a cosy Italian, laughing and joking over a bottle of house red, playing footsie under the table. Spoilt for choice for a room to go back to.

But he'd been distinctly off with her when, bumping into him as she left the theatre — he'd been standing outside in the cold sneaking a crafty cigarette — she'd mentioned her situation. All alone. No charges till the following day. Strange town. She'd practically spelled it out for him.

To say he'd cut her dead wouldn't have been true. But he'd definitely been distant and indifferent to her plight, more interested in getting his nicotine fix than fixing up a date. Finally, she'd had no alternative but to wave a feeble goodbye and leave him where she'd found him.

So now she was back at the digs, stuck in the poky room she shared with Kirsty, who was off eating Chinese with her dad somewhere, before spending the night in some fancy hotel with room service.

While the girls were away, she'd tidy up, that's what she'd do. All the sweet wrappers and the screwed-up tissues and the spare socks she found lurking beneath their beds she'd throw into a plastic bag, then wave under their noses when they returned, as a lesson to them that she was not their skivvy.

Without further ado, she started with Kirsty. Peering beneath her bed, Chrissie could see orange peel, a hairy hairbrush, a purple scrunchie and one half of a pair of slippers. There was something else there too. A wooden box, the size and shape of a shoe box, that was probably blocking her view of other stuff behind it. She dragged it out with the rest of the junk.

Chrissie wasn't a snooper by nature. And if the lid hadn't been half off she wouldn't have gone anywhere near it. But it was, and she did. And it was there, in among the newspaper cuttings of all the reviews of the show so far, that she discovered everything that had mysteriously gone missing since the start of the tour.

Titania's carved elephant, Lorna's charm bracelet, the combs, the lip glosses, her very own Snow Patrol CD she thought she'd left behind in Nottingham, a silver locket that she didn't recognise. And, finally, right at the bottom of the box, tucked inside a red woollen glove that Chrissie knew beyond doubt belonged to one of the twins, who'd been blaming the other twin for losing it for ages, was Maggie's bundle of twenty-pound notes.

# 3

Chrissie looked at her watch for the third time in a minute. There was only one hour left before Kirsty was due on stage and there was no sign of her. Somewhere a fire door opened with a creak, then clanged shut. Brisk footsteps echoed along a bare stone floor. Another door opened, then shut. Creak, clang. The footsteps gained momentum. Chrissie, terrified, glanced around for a prop. At this point a noose would have been good.

*Is this a dagger which I see before me?* Alas, no. It was one half of the baguette that Maggie had been quietly enjoying — not so quietly, actually — and had abandoned as soon as she realised the producer was heading this way. Chrissie couldn't believe she'd fled, leaving her to face the producer's wrath alone. When the chips — or in this case, the baguettes — were down, you certainly knew who your friends were.

More footsteps. A whole series of creaks and an entire raft of clangs. Death, when it came, would have been a release.

'Where is Kirsty? You've tried to get her on her mobile, I presume?'

'Ah — I — er.'

Chrissie opened her trembling hand to reveal Kirsty's iPhone, left behind in the girls' dressing room, As Chrissie had discovered when, in desperation, she'd rung the number only to be greeted by its muffled ringtone emerging from the pocket of the girl's pink towelling robe. Kirsty must have tucked it away there herself, then forgotten all about it, in her excitement at being whisked away so unexpectedly by her dad.

'The father, then? You've rung him, surely? Give me that phone. His number's bound to be on it. I'll ring the man myself.'

'No battery left,' Chrissie croaked. Her fault again. She'd rung it so often before she'd finally located it that it had managed to ring itself to death.

His eyes turned heavenward. 'Go and

look in the book, then. You wrote it down, surely?'

Oh, kill me now.

'You didn't, did you?'

If only he would shout. But it was this grim, calculating calmness that was so terrifying. The rictus smile, the dead eyes, which filled her with certainty that after this she would never get a job in the theatre again.

'I — he — Kirsty — it all happened so quickly. He just turned up and I thought — '

'Thought, did you? No, I really don't think you did.'

'I can play Puck,' Chrissie heard herself say. 'I know the part. The words, the moves, the songs. Everything. By heart. And I'm not much bigger than Kirsty, either. So fitting into the costume will be — '

'Enough!'

The producer sliced his arm through the air like a conductor silencing his orchestra with his baton. Or an executioner delivering a swipe of the axe.

'Before I sack you, Chrissie, I want to

be sure I've given you every chance. Don't think I didn't check up in the book before I dragged myself all the way over here.'

'Oh, I'm sure you did,' Chrissie thought.

'No, of course not,' she mumbled.

'So I already know who Kirsty's next of kin is, and who is and who isn't allowed to take her out of the theatre overnight.'

Oh, God! Kirsty's mum was down as next of kin, not Nat Granger.

'But,' he added, 'I'm a reasonable man. You have an hour. One hour. If she's not back by then, you will be going home. Now go and stand at the stage door and keep a lookout for her.'

Chrissie felt so deflated she couldn't even cry. What was there to cry about? The worst had already happened. Except it hadn't.

'You do understand that I'm under obligation to inform the mother about all this, don't you?'

Chrissie's knees began to wobble.

'She's on her way. And she's got a

couple of things she'd like to say to you.'

Now, *that* was the worst thing.

★  ★  ★

Eddie was outside, drinking coffee out of a paper cup. She got the impression he wished he hadn't seen her, which was a bit weird.

'I'm in deep doggy do-do,' she told him. She glanced at her watch. Twenty minutes had already disappeared. 'I've mislaid one of my charges and unless she turns up very shortly I'm about to get fired.'

'You?' Eddie raised an eyebrow.

'Yes, me. Why not me?'

Was she right and he really was being a bit off with her?

'Well, I'd have thought with your connections — '

'What connections?'

He didn't get a chance to reply. Here was Kirsty, hurtling along the pavement, arms full of carrier bags sporting the names of the classiest shops in Manchester.

'I never thought I'd be so glad to see

you,' Chrissie squealed. 'Wherever have you been? Give me those bags. You've got about half an hour to get into costume.'

'Ask Dad. What's in that bag is for you,' Kirsty panted. 'It's jewellery. I hope you'll like it.'

'I'll look later,' Chrissie said. Her first thought was that this was a sweet gesture and one she never would have expected from Kirsty.

Her second was that after what she'd just put her through, a diamond bracelet wouldn't have been good enough.

Nat Granger took a while to catch up. He was obviously someone who thought exercise meant flicking a button on his remote control.

'Got lost. Hopeless sense of direction. I am so, so sorry,' he said.

'You will be,' she told him. 'Your ex is on her way and she's breathing fire.'

She grinned at him. His face was a picture of doom. Turning to speak to Eddie, she noticed he was gone.

\* \* \*

Chrissie had banished Nat Granger to the auditorium. He'd already taken a phone call from Mandi Granger and Chrissie didn't want any trouble backstage before the show. Nor after, come to that, but she didn't think she had much choice in the matter as far as that went.

Now she was alone with Kirsty in the dressing room.

'Do you like it?'

Kirsty pointed to the turquoise pebble bracelet Chrissie had transferred from its exquisite gift wrap to her wrist.

'I love it. Nice and stretchy.' She tugged at the wristband to demonstrate. 'And the flower in the middle is so cool.'

'I knew that it'd be your sort of thing.'

'You know, Lorna had a lovely bracelet. Silver. Charms and stuff. Jangled when she moved. Did you ever see it?'

Kirsty became suddenly rather interested in an invisible spot on her chin.

'She had it at the beginning of the tour. But she hasn't seen it since Nottingham.'

'How many more minutes?' Kirsty sprang up from her chair and began to pace the floor.

The other girls were changing in the Fairies' dressing room.

Chrissie had organised the switch earlier. She and Kirsty needed a bit of space, was how she'd explained it. She'd expected a fight, but they'd fallen over themselves to accommodate her request, like they couldn't do enough for her. Made a change from Eddie's odd behaviour.

'Things do go missing, though, on tour,' Chrissie went on, refusing to be distracted by thoughts of Eddie Dawlish. 'Usually, they turn up again, thank goodness.'

She reached inside a drawer and pulled out the shoebox she'd discovered under Kirsty's bed. When she realised what it was, Kirsty's mouth dropped open and the colour drained from her face.

'I've taken the money out and given it back to its rightful owner. It's a lot of cash to leave lying about.'

She didn't mention the sleepless nights she'd spent worrying about it. This was about Kirsty, not about her.

'I didn't mean to steal any of these

things,' Kirsty whispered. 'I just wanted to keep them for a while.'

'Well, that's a start, I guess,' Chrissie said. 'But I'd feel a bit easier if I thought you weren't going to do it again.'

Kirsty's fingers alighted on Titania's carved wooden elephant. 'I just wanted something of my own,' she said, her fingers closing over it.

Chrissie was puzzled. Kirsty had more stuff than any kid she knew. So much stuff, it spilled out of drawers and wardrobes. So much that she never even noticed she'd left something behind when they moved on from one venue to another, until Chrissie came running after her with it.

'I thought if I took this it was like having a bit of Titania for myself,' Kirsty went on. 'She's always kind and everybody likes her.'

Chrissie swallowed hard. 'And the other stuff?'

Kirsty shrugged. 'Don't know. Same, probably. Everyone likes you and Lorna and Maggie, too.'

Chrissie struggled to get her head

round Kirsty's attempt at an explanation. 'So, you thought some of these other people's popularity would rub off on you if you took something that belonged to them?'

She was genuinely perplexed.

Kirsty stared up at her, her eyes threatening tears. 'I can't explain. Please, don't ask me.'

'Generally, people like other people because they're kind and helpful and they make other people feel good about themselves,' Chrissie said. She spoke softly. The last thing she wanted was to alienate the girl. 'You don't need me to tell you that you don't always act that way, Kirsty, do you?' she added.

Kirsty shook her head. 'I want to, though. It's just that something gets into me sometimes.' She replaced the wooden elephant back in her shoebox, her fingers lingering over the smooth wood.

'I know.' Kirsty seemed so vulnerable right now that all the resentment Chrissie had been storing up against her since she'd vanished with her dad simply evaporated. She just wanted to make it right for this troubled kid in whatever way she could.

'I want to give the stuff back, Chrissie,' Kirsty whispered. 'Will you help me?'

'Of course I will, sweetheart.'

'But I'm afraid of getting into trouble. I mean, if I return it, then they'll all know it was me who took it. What if they call the police?'

Chrissie rested a hand on Kirsty's shoulder. 'Just promise me you will never steal anything from another person.'

'I promise.'

That was all Chrissie wanted to hear. 'Good,' she said. 'Now, can you remember who everything belongs to?'

'I think so.'

'In that case, you've got five minutes to share the info with me before you go on.'

Kirsty widened her eyes. 'You'll put them back?' she said. 'You'd do that for me?'

'Only because I have your word that all this — pilfering — has ended.'

Kirsty's nods were so frantic that Chrissie had absolutely no doubt she meant it.

'And I want your word on something else, too,' Chrissie added. 'An apology to the other girls. No more snide remarks and nasty comments. And a bit of grovelling to the producer wouldn't go amiss, either.'

Kirsty grinned.

There was a sharp rap on the door. 'Three minutes.'

'There's your call, Kirsty. Now, what do you say?'

'Yes.'

When Kirsty smiled her face transformed. She was going to be a beautiful young woman, Chrissie thought. Once she got the inside right.

* * *

Chrissie's feelings of tranquillity and a job well done lasted for the length of time it took her to drop Kirsty off in the wings and walk back to the dressing room, whereupon she was pounced on by Kirsty's mother.

'How dare you! I trusted you to look after my daughter as I would have looked after her myself had I been here!'

Chrissie's blood had already begun to simmer as soon as she'd felt Mandi Granger's acrylic fingernail prod her in the shoulder. But as soon as she opened her mouth to speak, she began to seethe.

'Look after her? You? Oh, yes, an excellent job you've made of it, too!' It was time for a few home truths and the sooner the better.

An astounded Mrs Granger gasped at Chrissie's words. She stepped backwards — right on to the toes of her estranged husband. Good! The more the merrier! Chrissie relished the prospect of taking them both on.

'I hope you're not going to make a scene, Mandi,' Nat Granger said.

'No, she's not. I am,' Chrissie said. 'Inside, both of you.'

From the meek manner in which the two of them complied with her request, Chrissie guessed neither had been spoken to so firmly before. Snatching up Kirsty's shoebox, she tipped the contents out on to the dressing-room table.

'Stolen goods,' she said. 'There was a

bundle of notes to the value of fifteen hundred pounds, but that's already been returned to its rightful owner.'

Mr and Mrs Granger exchanged puzzled glances. It was obvious that Chrissie was going to have to spell it out for them.

* * *

Eddie didn't travel with them to their next destination, which was Sheffield. Someone passed her the message just as they were about to board the minibus. 'That's fine,' she told the messenger. 'He can do what he likes.' The messenger bobbed a sort of curtsey and scurried away and Chrissie wondered what on earth had got into her, talking to someone in such a hoity-toity manner.

Truth was, she'd been looking forward to catching up — not that she'd have uttered a word about Kirsty or the confrontation she'd had with the girl's parents, who, at the end of it, had left together, almost touching hands, heads bowed in contrition leaving Chrissie with the strong impression that they both knew they had an awful lot of self-examination to do. Everything that had gone on between Kirsty and herself was confidential, but there was bags of other stuff Eddie and she could have talked about.

But Chrissie couldn't remain down-hearted for long. Her spirits were soon lifted. There was that daft curtsey for one thing, like she'd been royalty, which she couldn't help tittering about. Added to that, the atmosphere on the bus between the girls was far lighter than the last time they'd travelled together.

At first, Chrissie put the cameraderie down to the girls' nice natures, after Kirsty's rather embarrassed apology to them. But when she saw they all had pebble bracelets similar to hers, she put two and two together. Kirsty had just bribed them into liking her and whoever said that never worked had never had anything to do with teenage girls.

The week in Sheffield sped by. No sooner had they arrived than it seemed time to pack up and move on, this time to

Leeds. No Eddie on that leg of the trip, either.

'Where is Eddie Dawlish these days?'

She was in Maggie's dressing room. Maggie was studying the *Financial Times*. 'Forget big boobs,' she said, when Chrissie asked her what she was doing. 'I've decided to start investing in my long-term future. Like I've heard you're doing.'

'Me?'

Inexplicably, Maggie tapped the side of her nose. Chrissie decided she'd been too long on tour. She was getting cabin fever. Never mind, only one more stop and that would be the end of it.

'Eddie's another,' Maggie said. 'Have you seen that bike he's riding these days? Who needs to be stuck in traffic when you can nip between lanes and get to your destination in half the time?'

'Eddie's got a motorbike?'

'Triumph Something-or-Other.' Maggie went back to the FTSE.

'Very impressive.' Chrissie was none the wiser. She was none the wiser about Maggie's other remark, either.

'What am I supposed to be investing in?' Chrissie didn't even have a pension, a fact which, on the whole, she'd so far successfully managed to push to the back of her mind.

'Oh, come on, Chrissie. Don't be coy! You've been spotted.'

Chrissie gave Maggie's remark some thought. Unfortunately, it wasn't ringing any bells.

Maggie lowered her newspaper again. 'You and Sir Anthony! Must say, I wouldn't blame you. The old boy will be worth buckets once he's shuffled off this mortal coil. Far more than he's worth alive.'

Sir Anthony? The most ancient member of the company? What on earth was Maggie on about?

'Everybody's talking about it,' Maggie went on. 'Even Titania's understudy caught you canoodling up to his waistcoat in his dressing room.'

Of course! She'd crept up on her searching for Maggie's money, so desperate she was ready suspect anyone, even Sir Anthony. Though not as desperate as

Titania's understudy, apparently, in her eagerness to make herself popular by spreading stupid rumours.

'I'll kill her,' she said.

'See, I didn't believe it, really. Not at first. Then I kept thinking, you do spend a lot of time with him.'

Chrissie gasped. 'You cannot be serious!'

She gave Maggie the censored version of what she'd been doing in the great man's dressing room, omitting any mention of turning it over for stolen money, but gladly putting her hand up to the waistcoat business.

'Sir Laurence Olivier gave it to him?' Maggie was impressed. 'Definitely mitigating circumstances, then. Of course you'd want to give it a sniff! And it's not like Sir Anthony was actually in it, is it? I never did like that understudy, you know. Always on the prowl for somebody to slander.'

'This explains everything,' Chrissie said. 'People have been treating me like royalty, lately. Opening doors for me, fetching me coffee. Someone even curtseyed the other day.'

Maggie giggled. 'Oh, God. How funny,' she said. 'That must be the Sir Anthony effect. You've gone from being slumdog to A-lister simply by association.'

Not with everyone, though. Chrissie thought back to Eddie's recent treatment of her. When he hadn't been avoiding her, he'd been speaking in riddles. What was all that nonsense he'd spouted when she'd told him she was about to lose her job?

'Connections! He thinks I've got connections.' She turned to Maggie, who was staring at her, mystified. 'Eddie Dawlish. Has he heard this blatantly false rumour about me, too?'

Maggie's puzzled expression dissolved and another one took its place. One of sheer wicked delight.

'So that's the way the wind blows, is it?' she said. 'Thank God for that. The poor man's been like a bear with a sore head recently. This'll cheer him up no end.'

Chrissie left Maggie wittering away to herself. Something about a midlife crisis. A motorbike as a substitute for unrequited love. Really, Maggie should stick to boob jobs and leave the psychology and the financial analysis to those better qualified, Chrissie mused, as she rushed off to find Eddie.

'I can't believe you thought I'd try and worm my way into an old man's affections just so I could stick the word 'Lady' in front of my name.'

Eddie was up in his little box. He flicked a switch, and then another one. 'Women do funny things when they reach a certain age,' he said mournfully.

She didn't know whether to hit him for lumping her together with all those other scheming minxes who'd bled men dry throughout the ages, or for suggesting she was a certain age.

'I'm sorry. I shouldn't have believed that stupid rumour,' he added. 'Of course you wouldn't do anything like that. You're much too nice.'

So, in the event, she didn't hit him at all but just said thank you. Barging into Eddie's inner sanctum had been a spur of the moment thing. She hadn't planned it nor had she planned what she was going to say. Now she'd said her piece, she felt ever so slightly stuck for words.

She looked around her, at the switches and the wires and all the other incomprehensible bits of equipment. This was a very small space. It was impossible to move a muscle without touching him.

To start with, she'd pulled back each time Eddie accidentally brushed against her as he moved around. But pretty soon she decided to stand still and let what happened happen. They'd wasted enough time already.

'Only one more venue,' Eddie said.

The look he gave her was a wistful one. Was he, like her, thinking that time was running out? A line from the play jumped into her head, a line so familiar in everyday parlance that she doubted most people knew it was Shakespeare who'd originally penned it.

The course of true love never did run smooth. He knew a thing or two, did old Shakey.

'Have you ever ridden pillion?'

Eddie's question caught her by surprise. You couldn't ride behind someone on a motorbike without clasping your arms very firmly about them. But, of course, Eddie must have known that.

'I haven't got a helmet,' she said.

'Don't worry about that,' he said. 'I've got a spare.'

'Hope you didn't get it specially,' she said, lying through her teeth.

He flicked a few switches, refusing to meet her gaze. But he didn't deny it.

# OFFSIDE

# 1

The hairdresser lifted a lock of Bella's thick, dark hair and peered at it. Bella had seen that look on the faces of the forensics' team at a crime scene when challenged with an inexplicable blood-stain. Detached, professional and only mildly curious.

'So you're not keen on aubergine, but have you ever thought about going blonde?'

The stylist's irritation at her client's inability to decide what she really wanted doing with her hair was beginning to seep through the mantle of bonhomie that was as much a part of her job as her snazzy scissors. Bella could hardly blame her, for it had been at her own instigation and no one else's when, some twenty minutes previously, she'd waltzed into the salon and announced that she fancied a radical change of image. Although it was beginning to feel like another decade.

Back then, when enthusiasm still hung in the air like the promise of spring, Sasha had plied her with a pile of magazines full of air-brushed models showing off the latest styles, waxing lyrical about how *this one* would suit the shape of Bella's face and how *that one* would add sophistication. But nothing really appealed.

'They're all a bit . . . ' Bella began, after she'd leafed through page after page, growing more and more dejected with each one.

She groped for an adjective that wouldn't be taken the wrong way. She rejected *fussy* on the grounds that it might reflect what she thought of Sasha's own ornate style. In the end, she settled on *high maintenance*.

'In my job I sometimes need to be somewhere at a moment's notice. I'm not sure if I can be bothered with all that teasing and blow-drying,' she muttered apologetically, adding silently, 'And some of these might catch people's eye a bit, too.' Not such a great idea if you're going under cover.

'Oh, that's right. You did say you were a

policewoman.' She couldn't have been less interested, obviously.

Bella Lockwood was a Detective Constable — the youngest DC Gratleigh nick had ever boasted. Not that she'd ever been one to blow her own trumpet — although maybe if she had, then things would be different.

It was partly because she felt it was high time her colleagues changed their perception of her that she'd finally taken the bull by the horns and made the appointment at Sasha's in the first place, spurred on by the smart new DC. He'd only joined their team five minutes ago, yet already had uniform running round to do his bidding as soon as he opened his mouth to make a request.

Perhaps if she swapped her trainers for a pair of heels and her jeans and battered biker jacket for a power suit they'd start taking her a bit more seriously, too, instead of confusing her with their annoyingly bossy teenage sister.

The new boy, Danny Glover, wore well-cut suits that flattered the figure of a man who looked like he worked out three times a week. His ties were probably made of silk, his shirts top of the range and he wore buttery suede shoes that screamed quality. Not surprising that everyone had started thinking he was running the station. Only this morning, WPC Smith had scampered off and got him a coffee from the machine even without him asking. When was the last time anyone had done that for her?

The skein of Bella's silent, fuming resentment at this new turn of events in office politics swiftly unravelled as Sasha thrust one more picture under her ungrateful client's nose.

'Have a look at this photo. That one there.'

Sasha jabbed an acrylic fingernail at one of a gallery of pictures exhibiting the local first division football team on a night out, many of whom were accompanied by their wives and girlfriends. Was there a collective noun for a group of WAGs? Bella wondered, as she contemplated the figure Sasha had picked out.

'That's Chloe Wiley — married to the goalie. There he is chatting to that new

144

forward they've paid a fortune for, Bradley Wade. Gorgeous, isn't he?'

Bella lacked the courage to disagree. Funny, a six-foot crim wielding a cricket bat in her face provoked no terror in Bella, merely contempt. But hairdressers put the fear of God in her.

'Very nice,' she said.

'My boyfriend doesn't think much of him, though,' Sasha went on. 'Says they could have got two Norwegians for the price of Bradley Wade. Off the pitch with injuries more often than not, so my Jim says.'

Bella cared the same about football as she did about having a hairstyle like this Chloe Wiley's. That is, not at all. With Sasha's commentary fading into a barely noticeable background buzz, she allowed her gaze to wander over the designer-clad, well-toned bodies of the Gratleigh team's WAGs. How did they manage to walk in shoes so high? Then there were the dresses that could only have been kept up by a huge effort of will. Everything about these women seemed posed and false. Yet, the men from whose arms they hung were still recognisably members of the human race — spruced up for a night out, fair enough, but none of them would have looked out of place on any high street on a Saturday night.

Did men really go for such artifice in women? she wondered. Did Danny Glover, for instance? No doubt he had his very own WAG, Bella thought gloomily. Though why she should care, she had no idea. He was about as much her type as this Bradley Wade was. Until you compared their eyes. There was nothing behind Bradley's eyes at all, but when it came to Danny . . .

'So what's it to be, then?'

Sasha's words brought her up sharp. Once more she'd caught herself dwelling on Danny Glover! This really had to stop.

'You know what,' she said, suddenly flustered. 'I think maybe just a trim, after all, if you don't mind.'

'I'll get you shampooed, shall I?' a thin-lipped Sasha sighed.

★   ★   ★

Bella made her way into the foyer of Gratleigh General. A hit-and-run victim had been brought in during the early hours of the morning and she was here to interview her. Early twenties and probably, from the way she'd been dressed, on her way home from a night out clubbing.

Before leaving the station, Bella had set a couple of uniform the task of checking the CCTV and she'd already checked the witness statements, such as they were, herself. Only one couple had seen something of what had happened, but neither could give a partial number plate or even the make of car.

In fact, they couldn't even agree on a colour. It was dark, one had said. And late, said the other. 'Yeah, and you were drunk and very likely had your mind on other things,' Bella had thought, masking her thoughts with a polite 'Thank you for your co-operation'.

Now she was badly in need of a coffee before she talked to the girl — provided she was in any state to talk, of course. So far, apparently, she hadn't even given her name. A bump on the head could have caused temporary amnesia that she still may not have shaken off, Bella reminded herself.

Someone she recognised was struggling to extricate a polystyrene cup from the coffee machine. She'd know those shoes anywhere. What was Danny Glover doing here, muscling in on her case?

She watched as he tugged a bit too hard in a bid to snatch his cup from the jaws of the machine. When some of the brown liquid leapt out on to his elegant trouser legs, she stifled a guffaw. Serve him right, butting in.

'Oh, dear. Need a tissue?'

Danny Glover stopped his ineffectual flapping about, looked up and, with a terse thank you, accepted the tissue she held out to him.

'Two DCs to interview one victim,' she said coolly. 'I could have sworn this was my case.'

Danny was clearly puzzled. Then his brow cleared as the penny finally dropped. 'I've just been visiting my gran, actually,' he said. 'Off duty. She's in Ward 3.'

Her previous smugness drained away with a whoosh. It was as if someone had suddenly pulled the plug out of the sink. She felt very silly indeed. Visiting a sick granny! How far ahead of her did *that* put him in the good-person league?

She mumbled an apology.

Danny's shrug in reply suggested misunderstandings happen even among friends. Did he think she was his friend? That meant she'd made a great job of covering her resentment, then. Oh, dear, now she felt even worse.

'This interview I'm about to do,' she said. 'You're welcome to come along if you've nothing better on.'

He made a big deal of giving her offer serious thought. Was he genuine or was he just milking it for all it was worth? If it was the latter, then it was only what she deserved, she mused.

His slow deliberation ended at last with a smile that reached his eyes and flooded her own insides till she thought she'd drown in it. There really was no getting away from it. Danny Glover had claimed her heart, whether she wanted him to or not.

'That's a very generous offer, DC Lockwood,' he said. 'Lead the way.'

Bella was giving Danny a lift, after what had turned out to be a no-show. Their interviewee had, quite simply, left, according to the anxious ward sister who, on their approach, had come flying to meet them.

It was hard to make sense of her garbled explanation, but the gist was that she must have packed her stuff and left the premises some time during the last hour, when her meds had been delivered by the very nurse who stood before them, flustered and apologetic to such a degree that Bella felt only sympathy for her.

Further questioning revealed that, in all probability, it was doubtful she'd left on her own two feet, being too badly shaken up and bruised, and that someone had probably picked her up. Whether it was at the young woman's request or whether she'd been removed against her will remained a mystery they hoped to solve back at the station with the help of CCTV footage.

'So, no name then,' Danny said. 'All we have to go on is the description.'

'Blonde, though not a natural one, average height, and a butterfly tattoo on her inner right thigh,' Bella said. 'Now, if it had been on her knuckles . . . '

'Quite,' Danny said.

The roads between the hospital and the station were thick with traffic, which gave Bella the opportunity to quiz Danny about how things were going in his new job. As slow as this road, was his answer. Nothing but break-ins, hoodlums and the odd domestic.

It was pretty much the same for herself, she said. She'd spent months getting to the bottom of some trouble at a teenage party. It was a relief that she'd finally collared someone and it was at last going to juvenile court.

'I've had one highlight, though,' he said, after congratulating her on her success. 'A brush with celebrity, even.'

Bella was intrigued. Gratleigh was hardly thick with celebrities, she said.

There was a poet, who'd been on the radio a few times, and someone from a boy band, though he probably didn't live here any more if he had any sense. Who could it possibly be?

'Know who Kurt Venga is?'

It definitely rang a bell. A footballer, played left wing for Gratleigh, that was it. She remembered him from one of the magazines at the hairdresser's the other day.

Danny's eyes lit up, impressed by her knowledge. 'So, you're a football fan, then?'

'Not remotely,' she said, cursing herself for having to disappoint him.

'At least you're honest. Most girls pretend they love it, when they really only love the players and the WAGs.'

She was glad she'd stuck to her guns. Now he saw her as an honest person, without the guile of other girls. The wistful bitterness of his comment suggested he wasn't lucky in love, though. Or was that wishful thinking on her part?

She'd already tried to summon up the courage to ask him if he had a girlfriend, but had stalled each time. The cool thing would be to wait for him to reveal his relationship status and not to pry. She settled on listening hard as he related his story about Venga, whom Danny had visited after getting a call that he'd been burgled.

'Must admit I pulled rank,' he said. 'Fortunately, the WPC who'd been told to make the visit was only too happy to let me go instead.'

That would be WPC Smith — Wendy — Bella decided, not without a pang of jealousy. As girly as her name, that one. Quickly, she dismissed her rival from her mind and concentrated on Danny's story.

It had been difficult to make out what Venga had said as his English was so poor, Danny said. Fortunately, Billy Morgan, the team manager, had been there for moral support. Or so Danny had initially presumed.

'Poor guy had invited over a few people he'd met at a club,' Danny said. 'Obviously lonely and desperate for company. Only, like Morgan said, he should have taken a bit more care in his choice of friends.'

'Oh?'

'At the end of the night when they all said goodbye, some of his stuff went with them.'

'Oops,' Bella said.

'I felt sorry for him, I must admit. Not only had he been ripped off, but he'd obviously been torn off a strip by Morgan for wasting police time by reporting a crime he'd more or less invited. Poor kid could hardly bear to look me in the eye,' Danny said. 'In the end, I had to tell him that a crime was a crime and he'd been right to call it in.'

Bella warmed to Danny further.

'Well, I hope it made him feel better,' she said. 'How's the investigation going?'

'Badly,' Danny said, 'Venga was so vague about everything. Couldn't give descriptions or remember names. Not even of the club where he'd met these so-called friends.'

'Couldn't or didn't want to?' Bella said, adding that perhaps he was just keeping something back.

She'd glimpsed Morgan on the TV

news. He was old school. If Venga's playmates had brought recreational drugs into his home, for instance, and if on top of that sex had been added to the mix somewhere, well, it was hardly surprising if Venga had kept his eyes fixed on the ground throughout Danny's questioning.

Perhaps they should make a return visit. Without Billy the Boss's knowledge this time, she suggested. Find out what had really happened. What about the missing girl? Danny wanted to know. Technically, Bella reminded him, there was no missing girl until someone actually reported her missing. Some people just didn't like hospitals and preferred their own beds when they were sick.

Danny frowned. 'Well, I'm not sure,' he said. 'Sounds a bit fishy her going off like that just minutes after that nurse told her to expect a visit from the police.'

'OK. Let's do it this way. We drop off the tapes, make a quick visit to Venga while we get someone to trawl through them for our butterfly tattoo, then drive back to the station to see what's turned up.'

It sounded like a plan, Danny said, finally relenting. Only, did she mind if they put Sport Radio on? He wanted to check the scores.

*   *   *

'So, have you got her?'

Kurt Venga, over six foot of prime athleticism, made even Danny look slight by comparison. He also made him look and sound vastly more intelligent, Bella thought, with that open, cheerful face and odd singsong accent.

They trailed behind him into his expensively yet sparsely furnished bachelor pad. Not even a picture on the wall, Bella noticed. The floor, the coffee table and the settee and chairs, by contrast, overflowed with stuff. Sports kit, shoes that had been kicked off, rolled-up socks, dirty plates and empty glasses. The usual detritus that made up the life of a single man, she guessed.

'I meant to tidy up,' he said, catching her look.

'No matter,' Bella said. 'Why did you say *she* just now?'

Venga's was one of those faces you could read like a book. When he stumbled over his explanation that he always got mixed up with *he* and *she*, they both knew they had him.

'Why don't you just tell us the truth about the night you were robbed, Mr Venga?' Danny asked him. 'There's no need to involve the boss in this, if that's what you're worried about.'

In the end, Venga had been a pushover. There'd been no party of friends, as Bella had suspected all along — just one friend — female. He couldn't remember her name, but he could describe her. Blonde, so high, and she had a tattoo of a butterfly near the top of her leg. She took his watch, his MP3 player and a ring. But he'd thought about it, and had decided to follow the boss's advice not to prosecute. If this came out he'd only end up looking a fool.

He wouldn't be the only one either.

Reluctantly, he'd let it be known that rumours were flying round the changing room that there'd been other victims among the team.

★ ★ ★

'So you agree we should interview the rest of the team and see if we can get Butterfly Tattoo's name at least?'

They'd been arguing about how to go about it ever since Bella had brought up the idea. Discovering that the hospital's CCTV had been down for an hour that morning — annoyingly coinciding with Butterfly's decision to go walkabout — meant they had less than nothing to go on.

'I said I agreed,' Danny said. 'I just think we need to go softly.'

'Because of the married men in the squad, you mean?' Bella glared at him. 'All boys together, is that it?'

Perhaps she'd been a bit too misty-eyed about Danny Glover. When push came to shove, he obviously put pack loyalty above loyalty to the person you'd made marriage vows to.

'I'm just saying we should use a bit of discretion.' Danny spoke patiently — infuriatingly so. 'If the married ones have had nothing to do with this girl then it would be unfair to arouse suspicion where none's due.'

He was so annoyingly reasonable.

'And if they have been involved with her?'

'Then it's up to them to talk to their wives. We're not the morality police.'

Bella stood up and brushed away the crumbs from the canteen bacon sandwich Danny had treated her to.

'We'll start with the single ones first,' she said.

★   ★   ★

Bradley Wade had seemed a good place to start, being the most eligible of all the bachelors on the Gratleigh team. He'd never heard the rumours about some girl ripping off his teammates, he said. He was the new boy and never heard any gossip. Bella couldn't help thinking he felt just the teensiest bit sorry for himself.

Two other single players, however, individually and shamefacedly admitted having brought the girl back home with them. Yes, she'd left with money, jewellery, other bits and pieces. No, they hadn't thought to report it. What, did she think they were nuts?

Next on the list was Jeff Wiley, the goalie with the pretty wife. Wiley had been seen leaving a local club with the girl by at least three other players. They'd agreed, albeit reluctantly on Bella's part, to interview the married men on club premises. None so far had admitted anything. Which didn't mean they were telling the truth, of course. Jeff Wiley was an exception, though. He'd clearly been expecting a visit, no doubt tipped off by the gossip that was going round about him.

'There's no point me denying it, is there?' Jeff Wiley looked like a man who'd been having a few sleepless nights. 'Chloe was away at her mum's with the kids — we'd been having a few differences. But we were working through them.'

The desperation in this affirmation would have moved a stone man. It failed to move Bella, however, who'd picked her side already.

'This girl came on to me at Jakki's. I'd had a bit to drink. Next thing she was coming home with me.'

He'd felt guilty ever since, he said. He'd never cheated on his wife before and the last thing he wanted was to screw up his marriage. Chloe and the girls were the most important things in the world to him.

It was ironic, Bella thought, that Butterfly had taken his watch as a trophy — an anniversary present from his wife.

Now she and Danny were sitting in the car outside the Wiley's family home, both deep in thought.

'He's told his wife the watch is at the jeweller's getting fixed,' Danny said.

Bella shook her head pitifully. 'The action of a desperate man,' she said.

Danny sighed. 'Where is our girl?' he suddenly blurted out.

'She's a thief,' Bella said. 'She's on the run.'

'I wish I was sure about that. I wish I was more sure about Jeff Wiley, too.'

'How do you mean?' Bella fiddled with the radio dial. Danny had had it on the Sports channel again. Sooner or later she was going to have to have words with him about this.

'I don't buy his Mr Nice Guy routine. *Oh, do come in, officers. I've been expecting you.*'

Bella admitted he did seem a bit creepy. All that stuff about how he loved his wife. Made her want to throw up.

'He loves her. And he doesn't want to lose her,' Danny said simply. 'And he's worried what the Press will do if they get a sniff of this.'

'They'll tear him limb from limb,' Bella said.

She thought a little longer. Danny was good at silences, which made thinking easier.

'What would a desperate man do to prevent a scandal and to keep his marriage together?' she said at last.

'Anything it took, I'd say,' Danny said.

'And if he failed the first time, maybe he'd try again.'

Bella mulled things over. What if this hit-and-run had been just a warning? Butterfly had got away with a few injuries on that occasion. But something had frightened her. Another threat, perhaps? Had she gone into hiding to save her own skin?

'I think we should take Jeff Wiley down to the station,' she said. 'Make things a bit more formal.'

Danny ran his fingers over his top lip.

'I think so, too,' he said.

# 2

In the interview room, Jeff Wiley flexed his laced fingers. Every so often he cracked his knuckles to emphasise a point whereupon Danny, sitting next to Bella, flinched.

'Look, I've put my hand up to the one-night stand.' His tone was urgent. 'But I swear I don't know anything about this hit-and-run business.'

He fixed Bella with red-rimmed eyes, the mauve shadows beneath them further evidence of lack of sleep. His solicitor sat beside him, sniffing the air for any trace of slippery tactics on the part of his client's accusers, like a hound on the scent of a rabbit.

Some briefs look shiftier than their clients, Bella thought, as once more Wiley cracked his knuckles and Danny flinched. Honestly, if that sound got to *her* so much, she'd have to say something. It was obviously impinging on his concentration.

'I've got a lot to lose by coming out about that night. It was the biggest mistake of my life. If my wife gets to hear of it, then it might be the end of my marriage.'

He closed his eyes and let out a small, fearful groan as the whole sorry night passed before him. He looked like a drowning man, Bella thought. But then he opened his eyes and rallied.

'You should be questioning those who *haven't* owned up, not innocent men like me that have.' Crack; flinch. 'I bet I'm not the only one who's fallen for this girl's charms.'

Bella suppressed a smile at this quaint expression. The idea that men were mere victims of wily women was still a current one, obviously.

'With respect, Mr Wiley,' Danny said, 'you came forward because you'd been spotted by two separate witnesses leaving the club with the young woman in question. It's hardly the same thing as admitting something freely, is it?'

The solicitor was starting to look agitated.

'You don't have to answer that,' he growled at Wiley. Then, turning back to Danny and Bella, he finally bared his fangs. 'You're going to have to let my client go, you know. You can't prove that he had any connection with this hit-and-run business apart from the fact that he took the girl home.'

Danny stroked his chin.

'You have to ask yourself who is the victim here and who the criminal.' A self-righteous tone had crept into the solicitor's voice. 'My client was robbed of a substantial amount of cash, not to mention a valuable watch.'

'That's right.' Danny checked his notes. 'An anniversary present from his wife, I believe.'

He fixed Wiley with a look that spoke volumes.

'Are you going to come clean to her?' he said.

Wiley looked startled. Obviously not then, Bella decided.

'Where does she think you are at the moment?' Danny persisted.

Wiley shrugged. 'She doesn't have a

clue. She's not the kind of woman who keeps tabs on me all the time.'

'Well, I expect that'll change when this gets out,' Danny said.

He looked like he was enjoying himself now — getting his revenge for the knuckle-cracking.

'What goes on between my client and his wife is really no concern of yours.' The solicitor set about shuffling his papers, in agitation. 'And if you're thinking of leaking any of this to the Press . . . '

'Wouldn't dream of it,' Danny said. 'They've got their own ways of ferreting out a scandal.'

'So, you going to let me go or what?' Wiley shot Danny a desperate look.

'You'll be pleased to know that yes, I am.' Danny stood up.

Wiley scrambled to his feet, relief and gratitude flooding his face. He shouldn't have been so quick to think he'd got away with it, though. What Danny said next took everyone's breath away.

'But I want you to go straight home and come clean to your wife.'

Wiley took a step back. His solicitor

gave a strangled cry of objection and laid a hand on his client's arm to steady him.

'You say you love her, right?'

Wiley nodded, suspicious as to where the question was leading.

'In that case, come clean or when she finds out about this from another source, she's going to want to know why you kept it back for so long.'

Danny held Wiley in a captive gaze. It was as if there was no one in the room but them.

'It won't matter how you explain it. How it meant nothing, or you were drunk or whatever. The trust will have gone,' he continued. 'And it'll always be there, eating away at her. She'll never fully trust you again.'

There was a pause while Danny's words sank in.

'Well,' the solicitor tutted. 'I really don't see . . . '

'Shut up.' Wiley shot the solicitor a steely look. 'The guy's right. She's everything to me. I can't risk her finding out from someone else.'

'What was it you said about us not being the Morality Police?'

Wiley and the solicitor had left, but Bella and Danny still lingered in the interview room, taking stock of how far they'd come, which, in truth, still wasn't very far at all. One down, eleven to go, Bella had said, hazarding a wild guess as to the number of men that made up a football team.

'You're right. Maybe I overstepped the mark back there.' Danny scrunched up his empty coffee cup and aimed it at the bin. 'Missed.'

She got the distinct impression that the subject was closed. There was still a lot she had to learn about Danny Glover where avoidance tactics were concerned, she decided. But when he'd spoken to Wiley about trust, and how easily it could be broken, it was hard to believe that Danny wasn't speaking from personal experience.

'So, what now?' she said, quickly changing the subject.

Danny shook his head gloomily. 'God knows.'

'Where do you think our girl is?'

'She could be dead for all I know.'

He strolled over to where his cup had landed, bent to retrieve it, took a few steps backwards and aimed again. This time he got his mark.

'Do you really think so?' She gave a shudder, hugging herself to ward off the dreadful images her police officer's brain threw up.

'Hey!' Danny looked alarmed. 'I didn't mean it. You were right earlier. She's a thief — a chancer who needs to keep a low profile. She's probably holed up at some friend's house till her wounds heal and she can get back to work robbing gullible guys who have more money than sense.'

'You saying you wouldn't fall for it, then?'

He met the challenge in her eyes. 'Me? No,' he said. 'As far as women go, I can read them like a book.'

'I expect you've had plenty of practice.'

He gave a half smile, neither denying it

nor concurring. He wasn't exactly saying mind your own business, but he might just as well have been, she decided. Well, two could play at that game.

Switching back into professional mode, she said, 'I'm just not as confident any more that she's OK, though.'

'How do you mean?'

'I dunno.' Bella was thinking aloud. 'I don't buy it that this girl *is* a chancer, frankly. I suspect she does her research — singles her victims out and goes for the flashy ones. *And* the ones with most to lose.'

A ripple of frown lines gathered on Danny's brow — a sure sign that he was giving her words serious thought, she'd learned.

'What if our girl was trying a bit of blackmail? And what if someone's decided to put a stop to it?' Danny was still frowning.

'I think we should get the Super's permission to put out a missing person alert to the media,' she said.

★   ★   ★

'So, let me get this straight. Is this young woman a villain or a victim?'

The Super's natty little black moustache twitched above his curling lip. He'd always done contempt excellently, Bella thought. She could almost hear Danny breathing beside her, as if gathering himself up to exhale a spurt of justification, if the boss said no. Or rather, when.

Superintendent Flood had hated the media ever since that story about him mistaking the Queen's lady-in-waiting for the Queen herself and ignoring Her Majesty completely when she got out of her car on a Royal visit once. The Press had had a field day with that one.

'She could be both, Sir,' Danny said, at exactly the same moment that Bella said, 'She might be neither.'

'Well, make your minds up,' the Super said.

It was stuffy in Superintendent Flood's office. Stuffy and stuffed to the gills. Barely a square inch of wall was just wall, and no horizontal standing surface was clutter free. He loved his trophies, did the

Governor, not to mention his certificates and his photos.

Bella followed Danny's gaze to one particular spot on the wall, where in one photograph Flood was shaking hands with a short, tubby man exhibiting an intricate comb-over.

One of his friends in high places, probably, Bella decided. In the photo, the Super was grinning from ear to ear as if he'd just won the lottery. Why was Danny so interested in it? she wondered, as the pattern of frown lines once more appeared on his brow.

Realising that now was not the time to let herself be distracted by Danny Glover, she turned her concentration back to the question in hand.

'As DC Glover has just said, it seems more than likely, from the nurse's description of the woman who let herself out of the hospital — or was possibly helped to leave the hospital, or who was even forced against her will to leave the hospital — and the description of those members of Gratleigh's football team who have, er, come into contact with her, that our thief and the victim of the hit-and-run incident are probably one and the same person.'

The Super blinked and sat back in his chair, as he did his best to unravel the tangled string of Bella's wordy argument. She threw Danny a wry smile to reassure him that she knew what she was doing. The Governor liked things complicated. Even simple things.

'I do not want the tabloids cluttering up my e-mail, or my phone lines or my foyer,' he said, after a minute had gone by, by which the Super appeared to have fully digested the information. 'I'm not agreeing to this. End of. Her going off like this is probably some great big publicity stunt. Next thing, she'll have her own reality TV show.'

Bella glanced at Danny for support.

'Doesn't reflect too well on Billy Morgan all this, Sir, does it?' His gaze returned to that photo.

So, that was Billy Morgan, was it?

'How do you mean?' The Super sniffed the air.

'Well,' he said, 'it might just look to the

media — and so by implication to the public — that Morgan puts protecting one of his boys before searching for a missing girl who could be in danger. And that he's putting a bit of pressure on his good friend the Super to help him out.'

Nice one, Danny! The Super cleared his throat. 'All right,' he said gruffly. 'Get that PR woman on the blower. Tell her to draw up a statement or whatever it is she does.'

★   ★   ★

'Thanks for the support back there.'

'No problem. I hoped you'd do the same for me.'

It was Bella's turn to get the bacon butties. She'd longed to suggest the pub instead of the canteen, to celebrate their victory. But she didn't want to give the wrong idea. It was impossible to have a private conversation when you could feel WPC Wendy Smith and her cronies looking daggers at you across the room.

Not to mention Danny's nose being stuck in the sports pages again. Every opportunity he'd had this last few days, there he was, eyes glued to the football reports. And she'd lost count of the skirmishes they'd had with the car-radio dial.

'Do you mind if I ask you something?'

Danny looked up from his paper. 'Go ahead.'

'What's happened to the smart suits and the fancy ties?'

Today, Danny was dressed in jeans and a crew neck. His jacket was about as scruffy as hers. He'd swapped the shoes for trainers too.

He finished chewing the last of his sandwich. 'To be honest, it wasn't me, all that dressing up. It felt uncomfortable.' He hesitated, choosing his next words carefully. 'I was sort of — hiding behind it, if you like,' he added, with a wry smile.

'I thought only girls did that,' she said. 'Well, some girls, that is.'

His smile grew broader. Some but definitely not you, it suggested.

'Anyway, what have you got to be afraid of?'

'Your reputation,' he said. 'Everyone I

176

spoke to before I arrived said what a great police officer you were. I didn't fancy my chances simply playing fairly. So I thought if I looked sharp people might think I *was* sharp.'

'Well, Danny, I'm flattered.' Bella allowed the full impact of his remark to sink in.

She was more than flattered, if truth were told. In fact, she thought she might burst with pride. She'd had the odd pat on the back and the occasional grunt of appreciation from colleagues previously, but verbal compliments upon the macho terrain of Gratleigh nick had always been — till now — the stuff of dreams.

Under the circumstances, she felt she really ought to return the compliment. She liked Danny in a suit. But she preferred him dressed like this — he looked more approachable for one thing. Less stiff and starchy.

'I feel I should say something about you, too, Danny . . . '

'Go on then,' he said expectantly.

But in the end, she couldn't quite bring herself to do it.

'You've got a bit of ketchup on your chin,' she said instead, handing him a napkin.

He took it and rubbed away at the ketchup that had been purely a figment of Bella's imagination, before returning to the article he was reading. He was soon as engrossed as ever. The upside-down headlines read, *INJURED WADE SCUPPERS GRATLEIGH'S CHANCES.*

'I've got a suggestion,' he said, when he'd finished it.

'Another cup of tea?'

'No. Not tea. I think we should go and visit Bradley Wade again.'

In the car en route to Wade's swish Quayside apartment, Bella probed Danny. Why was he so interested in revisiting Wade? The guy had shown no signs of nerves the last time they'd interviewed him, she reminded him. Just complete detachment and indifference at his Norwegian team-mate's plight. If he showed any emotion at all, it was self-pity because none of the other players had so far bothered to make him feel at home.

'A man with nothing to hide,' Danny said, as he negotiated a roundabout. 'Doesn't that strike you as odd, Bella?'

She considered it. 'Maybe. A little,' she concluded.

'What about you? What are you hiding, Danny Glover?' she wondered, with a sidelong glance at his profile. But Danny's eyes were fixed straight ahead, and he was giving nothing away. The consummate professional — that was Danny Glover.

'Most innocent people, when approached by two officers of the law, act a bit nervous at first, wouldn't you say? Even when they haven't done anything wrong.'

'I guess that's true. It's the hardened criminals who can smile and smile and be a villain,' she agreed.

He gave her a sidelong look of curiosity.

'Shakespeare,' she said. '*Hamlet*. Sort of.'

'This Bradley Wade, though,' Danny said, leaving Shakespeare behind. 'It's like nothing fazes him. You wonder if he's even listening half the time. He's just too glib for me.'

'He's a footballer, Danny.' Bella leaned across to change the dial to some nice classical music. 'That's how they talk. In clichés. End of the day. Back of the net. Game of two halves. Anything else defeats them.'

Danny said nothing as the car drew up outside their destination.

★ ★ ★

Bradley Wade was surprised to see them. He looked tired, Bella thought, a mere shadow of the airbrushed beefcake the celebrity magazines portrayed. Beside him, Danny Glover exuded rude health.

It was obvious from his first question that Danny had decided not to mince his words this time.

'You frequent the nightclubs, don't you?'

Wade had been snapped so many times either entering or leaving the local clubs he'd have been foolish to deny it.

'So you must have seen this girl hanging around?'

The footballer gave a guarded nod.

180

'And I can't believe that she didn't approach you. A good-looking guy like you.'

Wade's face registered a weary confusion as if his brain was stumbling to catch up with Danny's line of questioning.

'You'd be one of at least half a dozen others, you know — nothing to be ashamed of. We just need to find this girl before she rips anyone else off.'

'Look, mind if I sit down? I'm not feeling too clever.'

Bella spied a bottle of what looked like painkillers on the table, with a glass of water beside it. She gestured for him to take a seat.

'Thanks,' he said, as he collapsed. 'I've just taken something for the pain and, really, I need to go and lie down.'

'Just tell us what she took, Mr Wade,' Danny said. 'Then we'll leave you in peace.'

He stared vaguely ahead as if trying to recall something that had happened in the dim and distant past. Bella decided to give him a hand.

'Cash?'

He nodded.

'Watch? Mobile?' More nods.

'Laptop?'

An adamant shake of the head at this. No laptop, he said. He didn't possess a computer. As his eyes began to drift between their two faces, Bella realised they'd lost him.

Thank God for the painkillers, she joked, back in the car. They'd done a sterling trick of loosening Wade's tongue. Danny was about to reply when a call came through on the car radio.

There'd been a break-in at a flat on Donnell Street. A neighbour had heard movement in the night. Assuming it to be the occupier, returning after being away for some time, she'd turned over and gone back to sleep, relieved because she'd been on the point of ringing the police and sharing her suspicions about the identity of the missing girl she'd heard about on the radio and read about in the paper. Only, this morning, when she'd gone downstairs to deliver a parcel that had come for the occupier, she'd discovered the door ajar and the place completely turned over. That was when her suspicions started to bite even harder.

Finally, they'd got a name for Butterfly Girl. Tiffany Hughes, the neighbour had said.

★   ★   ★

Bella was miffed but she was expected in Juvenile Court all week. It was a complicated case and, although she wanted to be in on the search for Tiffany Hughes, she'd promised the three young victims of theft and assault at the teenage party that had been gatecrashed some six months previously and had finally got to court, that she'd be there for them.

Now she sat in the waiting room, waiting to be called by the Magistrate, her mind flitting between this case and the one she'd been dragged away from.

Someone was after something Tiffany Hughes possessed, obviously. Had they managed to retrieve it? In which case, she might be safe. Or had they failed? In which case she still needed to watch her back. And what about Bradley Wade?

Was he one more innocent victim or was he, as Danny suspected, hiding something?

Bradley Wade's picture on the cover of a well-thumbed and slightly out-of-date teen sport magazine caught Bella's eye. Picking it up, she leafed through the pages till she reached the interview with him that had been trumpeted on the cover.

It was set out as a Q&A-type interview. Favourite food, favourite holiday destination, the usual sort of thing.

Bella glossed over most of it. But her eyes were drawn to two answers in particular. In reply to *Favourite type of girl*, Wade had replied, *Blonde, long-legged, model-type*. Just like Tiffany Hughes, in fact.

More interestingly, under hobbies was listed *Surfing the Net*. Bella scrolled back to her memory of their recent interview. *No laptop*, he'd said. *I don't possess a computer.*

An usher popped his head around the door. The Magistrate was ready for her now, he said.

Bella leapt out of her seat, her mind spinning. Had she misheard him? She didn't think so. As soon as she got out of this courtroom, she'd be on the phone to Danny to check if she was right.

If Wade had once owned a laptop and no longer did, then where had it gone? Perhaps it had disappeared with Tiffany Hughes and all his other stuff. But if so, then why not say as much? You'd think he'd want it back. Unless, of course, he was a man with something to hide and Tiffany Hughes had discovered it on his laptop.

# 3

Bella tore through the station in search of Danny. What was the point of mobile phones if you didn't leave the damned things switched on? It was WPC Smith who finally pointed her in the right direction after she'd practically scoured the entire building. Probably been stalking him, she thought ungraciously. She was convinced Wendy Smith had a crush on Danny.

'There you are! I've been calling you ever since I got out of court.'

Danny had tucked himself away in one of the interview rooms. He was so deeply engrossed in his laptop, it took him a moment to respond. When he looked up at last, he smiled, looking genuinely pleased to see her. Bella's heart soared, leaving her breathless.

'You look flustered,' he said.

She felt flustered, but at least she could pretend it was work-related.

'I've just discovered something very interesting . . .'

'You want interesting? Then come and have a look at this.' Danny gestured her closer. 'Tiffany Hughes,' he said. 'Our girl's got form, Bella.'

Hardly surprising. Bella made another attempt to get Danny's full attention.

'Actually,' she began, but it was as if Danny hadn't even heard her.

'Says here she was a runaway. Three times before her fifteenth birthday. Made the break with her family at sixteen and has been nothing but trouble ever since. Fencing stolen goods, dealing, petty thieving, you name it . . .'

'Danny!'

'Looks like Butterfly Girl's more frightened of getting done for thieving than she is of whoever it was who tried to mow her down.'

'Danny! Will you please shut up and listen to me for a change!'

Finally she had his attention.

'Bradley Wade's been lying, Danny,' she said. 'He swore blind he didn't own a computer, remember? Yet, take a look at this.'

She slapped the magazine, still open at the right page, in front of Danny and pointed to the relevant part of the interview.

'You nicked this from the Juvenile Court's waiting room?' He shook his head in astonishment. 'Way to go, Detective Constable!'

'It's evidence. I'll replace it.' She snatched it back, aware of how easily he'd succeeded in goading her. 'So, what are we going to do next?'

Danny closed down his laptop.

'I'll get my coat,' he said.

But before they reached the main exit, the Duty Sergeant stopped them.

'You might be interested in this,' he said, shuffling out from behind his desk. 'There's been an anonymous call. From someone claiming to be speaking on behalf of Tiffany Hughes.'

'She knows something, for sure,' Danny said.

Bella agreed. 'I'll bet you any money the girl's got something on one of the players and she's about to go public,' she said.

Turning to the Duty Officer, she ordered him to put a trace on the call, a task he'd already allocated to WPC Smith, he said proudly.

'A nice little earner for Butterfly Girl, wouldn't you agree?' Danny said, as he put the car into gear. 'Something to kick-start her career as a Z-list celebrity.'

Bella leaned over to switch on the radio. Just as she suspected, it was on the local sports channel again. She was on the point of moving the dial when the name Jeff Wiley caught her in her tracks.

'Turn it up,' Danny said urgently.

Together, they listened to the news item. 'Jeff Wiley, goalkeeper for Gratleigh United, and his wife, former model Chloe Wiley, are flying out to Barbados for a short holiday,' the newscaster said. 'The couple earlier released a joint statement in which they acknowledged that they were going through some marital difficulties, but were confident that this time spent together would heal their differences.'

'Good luck with that one, mate,' Danny snorted, turning down the volume again.

'Cynic,' muttered Bella.

'Maybe with some cause.'

This was the first time Danny had given any hint that he might be open to further questioning about his personal life. And, also for the first time, Bella's curiosity finally got the better of her.

'Tell me to mind my own business . . . '

'Go on.'

'Well, you act single — none of this looking at your watch thing people who are one half of a couple always do when it's home time. But the way you talk sometimes, I'd swear you were a married man.'

Danny's expression suggested that she'd impressed him with her sleuthing.

'Bella, there's no use denying it,' he said. 'I have to admit you've got me bang to rights.'

Bella's heart plummeted. She'd so wanted to be wrong about this. From here on in, she would think of Danny Glover as nothing more than a colleague.

'Although, strictly speaking, I'm separated.'

Her heart gave a teensy-weensy hiccup of joy.

'And how do you feel about that?' She kept her voice neutral.

Without taking his eyes off the road, Danny told her. His words sounded glib, like they'd been well rehearsed.

'I thought we were happy. Trusted her with my life. Then she had a fling,' he said. 'I told myself I could forgive her. But it turned out I couldn't. Anyway, I've moved out.'

'I'm sorry,' she said.

'Don't be,' he said, upbeat. 'She broke my heart, but it's healing very nicely, thank you.'

Was he telling the truth or was this just male bravado? In the heavy silence that followed, Bella mulled over his words, then racked her brain to think of something appropriate to say. Fortunately, the radio announcer broke in over the music to save her the trouble.

'And just in — some breaking news, which will come as a huge shock to

191

Gratleigh United fans.'

Bella's antennae tingled once more and, at the exact same moment that Danny went to turn the volume up again, she shot out a hand to do the same. As soon as their two hands collided, they both pulled away as if they'd been scalded.

'In a shock announcement, popular manager Billy Morgan has resigned his position as manager of Gratleigh United FC.'

Morgan wanted to spend more time with his family, so the radio host said, a claim Danny dismissed with a snort as cynical as his previous one. When calls were invited from listeners on their reactions, Bella turned the radio off. They'd reached their destination and, besides, Bella had stopped listening.

Although they'd both immediately removed their hands after that initial accidental skirmish — Danny with a gruff apology — her own still tingled from his touch and her throat was dry. It was a relief to get out of the car and escape their close confinement. As they approached Bradley Wade's door, she hung back, seizing the opportunity to steady herself by deep breathing.

Bella and Danny were taken aback when, instead of Bradley Wade, a whey-faced Billy Morgan opened the door to greet them.

'You'd better come in,' he said, stepping aside to let them through.

He'd obviously been expecting them, then, Bella mused, as she trailed behind Danny into Wade's minimally furnished, yet expensively decorated lounge. Wade lay sprawled out on the sofa, dressed down in an expensive-looking tracksuit. Cashmere, Bella guessed.

Danny cut straight to the chase.

'So,' he said, addressing Morgan. 'You've resigned. I guess there's a reason?'

Billy Morgan looked as if all the fight had gone out of him.

'I'm finished,' he said, with a long sigh. 'If I don't go they'll sack me anyway. And, frankly, I don't care what happens to me. But Bradley needs help.'

'We'll come to Mr Wade in a bit,' Bella

said. 'Right now I'd like to hear your story.' Certain things were beginning to add up for her. 'What's your connection with this young woman, Tiffany Hughes?'

The look of contempt on Morgan's face at the mention of the girl's name told Bella all she needed to know. There was a connection all right — she hadn't imagined it.

'Was it you behind the wheel the night of the hit-and-run?' Danny was obviously one step ahead of her.

Morgan nodded.

'And what about her flat? Did you have anything to do with ransacking that, too?' said Danny.

Morgan gave another nod, almost imperceptible this time.

'What were you looking for, Mr Morgan?' Now it was Bella's turn.

'I did it for Bradley,' he said. 'To protect him.' Turning to Wade, he said, 'Go on, Bradley. You'd better tell them everything.'

Wade changed position, slumping forward and hugging his knees, giving the effect of a much smaller man than he really was and looking even more exhausted than the last time Bella had seen him. His eyes made a silent plea to Morgan. 'Don't make me do this,' they seemed to say. But Morgan's tight lips made it clear he'd said his piece for the time being. Now it was Wade's turn.

He struggled to speak at first, but then something changed. Maybe it was the sportsman in him, Bella thought, that made him realise that once he was through that tunnel there was only one way to go and that was forward on to the pitch. Win or lose.

'OK. I'll be straight with you,' he began. He uncurled his hands and spread them out, studying his fingers intently as he spoke. 'Things haven't gone so well for me since I've been at Gratleigh.'

Danny nodded. 'Six matches, no goals, two missed penalties, taken off at half-time on at least three occasions, stretchered off with a groin injury once and a recurring ankle injury twice.'

So, he hadn't been wasting his time reading the sports pages. He'd actually been obtaining and collating vital evidence.

Wade nodded miserably. 'Sport's my life. Always has been,' he said. 'I don't know what to do with myself when I'm injured. I was on painkillers before I came here, thanks to that ankle injury. Then the doctors wouldn't give me any more. Said I should rest up. But I'd just signed this deal. How could I?'

He glanced at his boss, nervously, as if he knew how it might look — that he was accusing Morgan of forcing him to play when he was clearly unfit.

'It was me that kept insisting I was all right to go on,' he said, correcting the impression. 'Billy never made me or nothing.'

'I didn't argue though, did I, when you refused to rest up like you'd been told.' Billy Morgan leapt to his centre forward's defence. 'I turned a blind eye to the pain you were in and never thought to ask you how you was getting through the training sessions.'

'And how *were* you getting through them, Mr Wade?'

Morgan answered for him when it grew clear Wade was struggling to make his admission. 'Prescription pills bought online,' he said. 'Spending a fortune, he was. Eating them like sweets.' His voice grew urgent. 'Can't you see the lad's got a problem? It's gone way beyond pain control. He's addicted.'

It certainly explained a lot. Bella recalled the pills on the coffee table on their last visit and the way he only appeared to be half listening when he was spoken to. Then there was his unhealthy pallor and poor posture — characteristics hardly compatible with a sportsman at the top of his game.

'I had to do something when he came to me and told me about that girl. How she'd come back here with him and left in the morning with his laptop. Everything was on there! All the details of his transactions with the pharmaceutical suppliers he was dealing with.'

Bella and Danny exchanged glances.

'Girls like that are rubbish,' Morgan went on. 'And I'd have made a better job of getting rid of her had I known she wasn't going to leave it at Bradley, but planned to work her way through my entire squad.'

'There is a trace on a call from someone who's probably acting on her behalf,' Danny remarked. 'Whatever she's got on your boys she won't be allowed to profit from it, rest assured. She's a thief, after all. However, that doesn't excuse what you've done, Mr Morgan. I'm going to have to arrest you for an attempt on Miss Hughes' life, as well as breaking and entering.'

Danny read the caution.

'It's over for me,' said Morgan, when he'd finished. 'Just get some help for Bradley here. He's still got a career ahead of him.'

Bradley Wade was looking even more wretched now than he had done earlier. He'd broken out in a sweat and he was doing his utmost to control the trembling in his limbs. The sooner he was booked into rehab the better, she thought. Just then a text came through on her mobile.

*If you're near a TV switch on to the rolling news channel,* it said.

She flashed Danny the message.

'You couldn't put your TV on, could you?' Danny asked Bradley, now equally intrigued. 'The news channel?'

Bradley obliged with the flick of the remote.

'And finally.'

The newsreader's amused face filled the wide screen. If that was HD, Bella decided, then she hoped to God she wouldn't have to appear on TV any time soon. Not even the slightest imperfection had a place to hide.

'When twenty-one-year-old Tiffany Hughes — who describes herself as a glamour model on her Facebook page — invited members of the Press to the foyer of Gratleigh Lodge this morning, where she promised to release a statement that would, in her words, lift the lid on a scandal that involved not only a very significant member of the town's first division football team but his manager, too, she got more than she bargained for. In fact, she got arrested.'

'What — !' Danny edged closer to the TV.

Bella shushed him as the newscaster

moved his story on, setting the scene — the cameras, the lights, the flowers and Miss Hughes herself, about to blow the whistle on Bradley Wade.

'Is he going to show it?' she wondered aloud.

Yes, it seemed he was. There was Butterfly Girl herself, quite a looker, if truth were told, standing at the microphone.

It was just as she opened her mouth to speak that a very irate police officer marched on to the stage and, in full view of everyone, cried, 'Right! That's enough of that! Tiffany Hughes, I'm arresting you for the theft of . . . '

The rest of the caution was drowned out by Danny and Bella's cries of amazement.

'Good on you, WPC Wendy Smith!' Danny whooped.

Bella wished she wasn't but she was actually very impressed by Wendy. Single-handedly, it appeared, she'd stopped Tiffany Hughes in her tracks.

'I am amazed,' Danny said to the assembled company.

'Wendy? Is that really her?'

Wade's question, so unexpected, drew everyone's attention back to him. His face, just a few moments ago so lifeless, seemed suddenly lit up. Did he know her? Bella wanted to know.

'We went out together all through school,' he said. 'Then I got signed and dumped her. Thought I was too good for her.'

'Well, it looks like she's still carrying a candle for you, if not a bloomin' great spotlight,' Danny said. 'Traces the agent, finds out where Tiffany Hughes intends to make her splash and hotfoots it to the hotel to make sure it never happens.'

All in one desperate bid to save her childhood sweetheart's reputation. So, it never was Danny she fancied. Danny was merely the man to ask about Bradley.

Wade was still staring at the screen, although the story had long since ended, and had now been replaced by the weather forecast. Imminent storms ahead, but a period of prolonged quiet weather to follow, so Bella observed.

'We was really good together,' Bradley said wistfully.

'Well, you never know,' Bella offered. 'Get yourself sorted out and maybe you still could be.'

★ ★ ★

A week had passed. Bella was catching up with the Sunday papers after a day spent blitzing her flat. There were pictures of Bradley waving to well-wishers as he went through the doors of the prestigious rehab clinic he'd checked himself into. Pictures of Jeff and Chloe Wiley smiling for the paparazzi back home after their make-or-break holiday. From their body language, Bella guessed it was the former.

She wasn't remotely interested in any of the nonsense about Tiffany Hughes, who'd already fulfilled her dream of being splashed across the tabloids — she simply didn't want to give her the pleasure.

Nor did she care much about Morgan. After all, two wrongs had never made a right. Let the courts deal with him. She'd already had words with Danny about the lengths some people would go to to protect their investment, which was all Bradley was to Billy Morgan, she was convinced, or he'd have acted on the signs of drug dependency long before he did.

Danny had quoted those famous words about football not being a matter of life and death, but of being much more important than that. Ha, ha, very funny, she'd said in reply, and thanked God she was a girl and thought differently.

It must have been all of half an hour since she'd last thought of Danny. They'd been working on different cases all week and had only glimpsed each other in passing. She missed him, but she'd made her mind up. He might have moved out of the matrimonial home, but a man who can move out can also move back in.

Her doorbell rang and she fought her way out of the pile of papers to answer it.

'Danny!'

'Sunday lunch!' Danny, dressed in jeans and a comfy sweatshirt, held up a brown paper bag that obviously — from the aroma wafting up from it — contained an Indian takeaway. Under his other arm were a couple of bottles of beer.

She felt flustered, wished she was wearing better clothes and had put on some make-up.

'It was a mistake,' he said, realising how he may have caught her unawares. 'I should have rung first. Only — '

'Only what?' There. She'd put him on the back foot now.

'I've missed you. And I think you've been keeping out of my way. And I want to know why.'

'You're married, Danny.'

'Separated.'

'I'm not looking for anyone on the rebound.'

Danny handed her the bag.

'Well, that's good,' he said. 'Because I'm not on the rebound.'

She had a choice. She could send him away or she could invite him in, eat his curry and drink his beer and send him away later. Funny, but neither choice seemed to fit the bill, really.

'Have you got popadoms?' she said. 'And lime pickle? Because unless there's lime pickle — '

'Bella,' he said, stepping over the threshold at last, 'I've got everything a girl could wish for.'

'We'll see about that,' she said.

After all, it was early days yet.

# CHRISTMAS COMES BUT TWICE A YEAR

# 1

Darius had been waiting at the bus stop for twenty minutes. Pretty soon he was convinced his feet — inadequately shod in the fake designer trainers he'd been persuaded to buy from the Saturday market — would drop off with cold. He dug his hands deeper into the pockets of his thin, cheap jeans.

Back home, the geography teacher had taught them that, unlike their own country, England possessed a temperate climate. He'd forgotten to mention the damp that thinned your blood to a trickle and seeped away your energy, so that even though you wanted more than anything to speak English well enough to get a good job back home, getting out of bed to go to class on time proved a challenge.

Today Darius had rolled over and gone back to sleep. Then, when he finally coaxed himself out of his warm bed with the promise of a shower and a good breakfast, he'd discovered there was no hot water left, and that the bread and milk he'd bought last night from the twenty-four-hour supermart had mysteriously disappeared.

He cursed his housemates one by one. Tomas and Jerome; rich Swiss boys with bankers for fathers. So indifferent to how well they did in the weekly tests that most days they didn't even bother turning up for lessons. Takumi, the Japanese boy, who spent every weekend discovering the delights of one European capital after another. And Cosmo, the smooth Italian who used the language school as a dating agency and, on the day Darius had brought home his trainers, had told him he'd been properly had.

He hated them — for making it impossible for him to do his homework in the evening and keeping him awake at night with their loud music. For the mess they made and never cleared up, and the time they took in the bathroom.

Most of all, he hated them for the casual way they treated their possessions. Leaving their expensive phones on the living-room floor for people to stand on and break. Spilling wine down their cashmere sweaters then throwing them into the washing machine from where they'd later emerge shrunken and unwearable. Ordering takeaways, then leaving them because someone rang up and suggested a more interesting alternative. No, he had to get out of that house if he was going to survive in this God-forsaken country.

Pulling his jacket collar up around his ears, Darius peered out from the shelter to see if there was any sign of a bus. Nothing. Only a young girl teetering down the street in a ridiculously short skirt and high heels, pushing a buggy that veered dangerously from side to side, under the weight of shopping bags. He could be here for another hour at this rate.

★　★　★

Carly's day so far had had an equally unpromising beginning. No milk, no cereal and only strawberry jam to put on

Lily-Rose's toast. She'd had no alternative but to get dressed, shove Lily-Rose into her all-in-one over the top of her jim-jams, put her in the buggy and make the five-minute trip to Rezia's.

At the time, it had seemed a good idea to pick up a few extra things. Rezia was doing a three-for-two on selection boxes and a buy-one-get-one-free on tinned ham, so it would have been madness not to stock up for Christmas. As soon as she got home, she'd ring her mum and insist she came round for Boxing Day tea and brought Nan with her. She was not spending a single moment of the Christmas period alone, even if it meant inviting tramps in off the street.

If she ever did get home, of course. Clunk-clunk-clunk all the way to Rezia's and clank-clank-clank all the way back. It was embarrassing, the racket Lily-Rose's buggy made. The lad in the bus shelter she'd just passed hadn't been able to tear his eyes away from them — and it was no use telling herself it was her own chassis his eyes were glued to.

On top of everything. Lily Rose who'd

started in first gear with a muffled whine as soon as they'd left the shop, had gone up the gears with every bump and lurch the buggy had made since. Now she was at full throttle. Carly wasn't blaming her daughter, who was usually as good as gold. But it just added to the assault on her ears.

She felt a sudden change of pressure beneath her grip. It was as if the buggy had had enough and simply crumpled. No matter how hard she pushed, it refused to budge another centimetre. Lily-Rose's howls reached stratospheric proportions. Carly was just about to join in, as the full implication of her plight seeped into her tired, cold, hungry brain, when she was distracted by footsteps behind her.

'Please. I saw what happen. The wheel. It go into road and under car. Buggy kaput, I think.'

Carly raised her face to the stranger's. He was tall, dark, handsome. Her knight in shining armour. Her bottom lip trembled. Two big fat tears welled up, one in each eye, and coursed down her cheeks.

'Don't cry. I help you. You take baby. I take bags. And stroller. Tell me where you live. We go together. OK?'

★  ★  ★

At Burton's (*Purveyor of High Quality Bread and Cakes since 1972*), the last of the trays had been wiped, the floor mopped and it was almost time to shut up shop for another day.

'I don't know, Jilly. All that education and still nothing proper to show for it at thirty years of age. Living on a houseboat when you could have your own flat, riding a pushbike instead of driving a car. Not to mention working part-time for an hourly rate instead of a proper salary.'

Eileen Burton ran a damp cloth over the counter vigorously.

'What was all that education for?' she added. 'Honestly, I'm just lost for words sometimes.'

'Really, Mother? Can't say I'd noticed.'

Jilly spoke through a mouthful of mince pie. She needed something to counter the tedium that listening to this well-worn theme of her mother's always induced in her, and the mince pie had been going begging because a bit of the crust had fallen off.

She wouldn't mind, but she'd only popped in to ask if there was anything her mother needed from town. In future, she'd time her arrival to coincide with one of the thrice-daily raids the kids from the local comp launched on the shop. That way her mother would be far too busy warning would-be shoplifters off her croissants to concern herself with the many flaws — as she saw them — in her daughter's character.

Jilly was tired. She'd been called out by the police in the middle of the night to act as interpreter for a South American migrant worker who'd taken a wrong turning after one too many beers and ended up in a part of town where strangers with money in their wallets were fair game. By the time she got back to her bed the night was all but over and it was practically time to think about getting up again.

To appease her mother, she decided it

would be wise to trot out how much she appreciated everything Eileen had done for her. Which she genuinely did, most of the time. She was a great role model, Jilly said, running the baker's business single-handedly after Dad had died, up early and in bed late, with hardly any help to speak of. She'd managed to succeed where many corner shops had gone under, due to the competition from the out-of-town supermarkets and the local predilection for the poor-quality wrapped muck that Rezia's Mini Mart stocked.

'It was your determination that made me realise how important it is to set your own goals, not simply follow the direction others point you in,' she said.

Her eyes strayed over to the doughnuts on display. Now was probably not a good time to suggest what a nice gesture it'd be if her mother offered her one out of the goodness of her very generous heart.

'I like what I do. I'd get bored doing the same job day in, day out. Dividing my working week between four jobs means I get to have my cake and eat it.'

'Four jobs is it, now? I know about the

language school and the police interpreting, but what else have you taken on?'

'A bit of private coaching. Kids of parents who think they can buy brains for their largely unteachable offspring. And a bit of voluntary teaching at the Bangladeshi Women's Centre.'

'Voluntary work?'

The look her mother gave her suggested she thought Jilly had finally and completely lost the plot. Jilly suspected her mother, a Yorkshirewoman by birth, had the words 'If tha' ever does owt for nowt, do it for thissen' tattooed on her heart.

'Look, Mum, do you mind if we change the subject? 'Tis the season to be jolly, after all. Peace and goodwill to all men and all that. Speaking of which, that was a very superior mince pie, if you'll allow me to say.'

Her mother coloured up at the praise. Jilly felt relief that this little bit of flattery had done the trick.

'Ground almonds in the pastry,' she said. 'Go next door to Rezia's and all you'll get in your mince pies there is floor sweepings.'

Jilly grinned.

'Talking of which, though, I should tell you about these fake twenty-pound notes that are going round. Rezia's had the police in.'

'No way!'

It was very rare for anything exciting to happen on the Burroway estate. But if there was any gossip, then Jilly could be sure her mother would relay it in all its juicy detail. Last week, it had been the story of the little boy whose bike had been stolen — taken from him in broad daylight by a gang of thugs, apparently.

Worse, the poor kid had been sacked from his paper round because he no longer had any transport, a job he relied on, so Eileen had said, because his mother hadn't been able to work for months due to a chronic asthma condition.

But forged twenty-pound notes! Now that was something else altogether.

'I've been forced to put up a notice advising customers that I'll no longer be accepting notes of that denomination until the counterfeiters are caught.'

Eileen gave a cursory nod towards the noticeboard where the notice, written in red, jostled for space among the adverts for babysitters, second-hand goods and rooms to let.

'Nice one, Ma,' Jilly said.

At that moment, the door swung open and the anxious face of a young woman appeared round it.

'You still open, Eileen?'

'Well, I never turn away a customer, dear, even though I've nothing left — except a couple of loaves I could let you have half price and a jam doughnut for your Lily-Rose. To be honest, you'd be doing me a real favour if you took it away. I'd only end up wearing it on my hips next week if I took it home. Ten pence do you?'

Jilly marvelled at the contradictions in her mother's nature. Only five minutes previously her face had expressed dismay when Jilly told her about the voluntary teaching she'd taken on. Now she was practically giving away bread and cakes she could have taken home herself — or, better still, given to Jilly who, as usual, didn't have a thing to eat on her houseboat that wasn't either past its sell-by date or completely unfanciable.

The girl gave a grateful smile, then flushed bright crimson when she realised Jilly was in the shop. Jilly studiously ignored her, turning her attention to her mother's overwrought message on the noticeboard. She'd misspelled 'counterfeiters', she noticed.

'I wasn't coming in for bread, Eileen. But if you were only going to throw it out . . .'

'Consider it yours!' Eileen reached under the counter for the two fat loaves and leftover doughnut. Jilly suspected Carly was a regular visitor at this time of the day and that their previous conversation had simply been a formality to save the girl's face.

'I just wondered if I could put this notice up on your board.' Carly withdrew a card from her bag. 'Thought I'd try and rent out me spare room. You know, make a bit of money for Christmas.'

'By all means, Carly. Stick it on the board if you can find a space. Where is

Lily-Rose, by the way? With her gran?'

Carly nodded. 'I can't be long. Mum goes berserk if she misses a minute of Paul O'Grady and Lily-Rose prefers *CBeebies*. I would have brought her along. Only the wheel fell off me buggy today, so I'm kind of stranded.'

'Look, Mum, I'll leave you to it,' Jilly said, on her way to the door. 'I'll catch up with you later.'

It was already dark outside. She didn't really fancy going into town now anyway.

★ ★ ★

Shelley Lansdown, Police Community Support Officer, was heading back to HQ. In her head the term suggested a swish office in a light and airy building surrounded by the latest in surveillance equipment and edgy designer furniture. The reality was less glamorous, unfortunately — a tiny, windowless room, freezing in winter and boiling in summer, situated next to the men's toilets at Burroway Community College.

The only good thing about its situation

was that both her kids, Heather and Nathan, were students at the college, so rarely a working day went by without her bumping into them. Not that they ever acknowledged her in her uniform with anything more than a gruff expression of recognition. Shelley quickly learned not to take their reaction personally, though, after Heather had pointed out that it wasn't Shelley so much as the uniform they felt obliged to blank when in the company of friends, and Shelley quite understood.

Her own mother, Ruby, who'd always had somewhat eclectic and highly personal sartorial leanings, had provoked a similar response in Shelley, when younger. Still did, actually.

Shelley was responding to a mysterious text. Up until a couple of weeks ago, she'd have said the other good thing about the freezing box she called HQ was that she got to share it with Guy Quinn, who was not only the Community Beat Officer and her line manager, but her very hunky boyfriend. Though maybe boy was pushing it a bit, even if forty was the new thirty.

*Something to show you. Hurry back*, had been the message. Her heart had lifted when she'd read it. Could it be, with Christmas looming, that Guy had decided now was the time to take their relationship to another level and he'd gone out and bought her a ring?

What if, while she pedalled furiously to beat the threatening rain, he was even now sweeping the office floor in preparation for going down on one knee? Guy had been behaving very oddly recently. But, if the reason for his spells of silence and absent-mindedness had been because he was trying to figure out how to broach the subject of a proposal, then she was prepared to be generous in her forgiveness.

What answer would she give him, though? She liked him. Very much. As a rule. He made her pulse race when he walked into a room. The kids accepted him. Even Ruby — who'd never been too keen on the police after many run-ins with them when she'd been a protester at Greenham Common — thought he was a nice man.

Nothing fazed or flustered him. Single-handedly, while an officer at the Met, he'd fought off three burglars and gone on to arrest them. He'd been terribly badly injured, however, and the incident had affected him so strongly that soon after he'd left the Met and moved out of London altogether, when he accepted the much safer job he had now.

Shelley had met him on her second day as a PCSO and hadn't really known how to take him. He'd been a puzzle ever since. With her first husband, Glyn, who'd sadly died when the children were much younger, she'd always been able to read his mind. Of course, the fact that they'd been together since school might have had something to do with that.

But with Guy, she just never knew how he felt. Was he already regretting his move and bored with Burroway and the mundane form filling and report writing so much of his new role entailed?

No matter how much she studied him, she still didn't have a clue half the time what was going on in Guy's mind. Part of the attraction, certainly — but at moments like this, as she walked through the college grounds, greeting many of the students with a friendly nod, cause for a great deal of concern, too.

★ ★ ★

Darius had cleared a space on his bed by flinging his dirty washing on the floor. Now he was ready to make a start on his homework.

*An Unusual Event.* That was the title Jilly had set for their homework this week. The whole class had groaned. Not Darius, though. He knew exactly what he intended to write — had planned it all the way home on the bus and all through his usual meal of spaghetti and sauce from a jar.

Of course, he didn't have the English to write about everything that happened from the moment he'd run to the girl's aid when the wheel of her stroller had fallen off. He must learn to write 'buggy', though. Stroller was what the Americans said, Carly had told him, as between them they'd struggled back to her house with all her bits and pieces, not to mention the baby, too.

He'd never spoken so much English all at once as he had that morning. She was nosy, she'd said, laughing as she spoke. He mustn't mind her asking all these questions, but she had spent so much time on her own since her boyfriend left that she could just about talk for England.

He wanted to tell her he was lonely, too. That his housemates were pigs and hated him because he was serious and wanted to do well, and wasn't interested in partying and wasting time like they were. But he didn't have the English. And besides, even the thought of his housemates didn't seem so bad now that Carly was smiling at him and asking him in for a cup of tea, as a thanks for saving her life.

Cosmo would have been in like a shot. The tales he told of his female conquests were many and lurid and Darius was certain none of it was made up. But Darius wasn't Cosmo and he'd blown it in the end. Made some excuse about school and not wanting to be any later than he already was.

Carly had looked disappointed, which made him feel happy. 'Another time,' she'd said, and like a fool he'd just answered, 'Yes, another time,' and gone on his way.

'What kind of idiot are you?' he could imagine Cosmo asking him, before going on to tell him exactly what he himself would have done in the same circumstances.

From somewhere across the landing, the insistent sound of rap music started up. Darius groaned and threw his pen on the floor. The sooner he found another place to live the better.

★   ★   ★

'A puppy! But, Guy, how on earth are you going to look after a puppy with the hours you work? You said yourself it was because he was so unmanageable that your next-door neighbours asked you if you'd take him off their hands!'

Not that Guy had needed to tell her

anything about the puppy's exuberant nature. The black Labrador, who answered to the name of Dog, had leapt up at her within thirty seconds of her opening the office door, licking her to death.

'High-spirited, I think I said, Shelley, to be fair,' Guy said, raising his voice over Dog's, so she could hear him.

'Whatever word you choose, it's just not practical,' Shelley said, covering her ears with her hands.

'Well, that's where I thought you could come in. And the kids. And Ruby, even, if she's got a spare minute.'

Skilfully, Guy wrestled a crime report from between Dog's jaws. Shelley looked on, horrified. She was rubbish with dogs. And if it misbehaved like that when Ruby was in charge of it, it would end up in the canal!

Dog, seemingly exhausted now, lay on the ground, its front paws stretched out. Now he'd stopped barking, he was quite sweet. He was all out of proportion, Shelley noticed, and his eyes, treacle-brown and trusting, were almost as big as his paws.

Her thoughts turned to Heather and Nathan. They'd always wanted a dog and, concerned about the mess it would cause, she'd never let them have one. But Dog, presumably, would be living with Guy.

'You'd just want us to walk him, would you? Only I wouldn't want him in my house and there's no room for a dog on Ruby's boat.'

Dog, head on one side, gazed up at her with melting eyes, and gave a yelp, as if promising to be on his best behaviour.

'I knew I could count on you, Shelley,' Guy said. 'Now, I just need to give you a few pointers about the best way to manage him.'

Oh, well. And to think she'd already started thinking about her wedding.

★   ★   ★

Carly had always been a light sleeper since Lily-Rose's arrival. It had started when she'd brought her back from hospital and Steve, Lily-Rose's father, had insisted that getting up in the night when she cried was Carly's job, it being a well-known fact that women had a much better grasp of nurturing infants than men did, who were better suited at hunter-gathering.

The only hunting Steve had ever done was through her handbag for fags and all he'd ever gathered was loose change from down the back of the settee. When he'd gone back to his mother's, moaning that Carly was no fun any more, the habit of waking at all hours of the night stayed with her.

If anything happened to Lily-Rose, then Carly was totally responsible. Was it any wonder she fretted herself awake imagining fire, theft and acts of vandalism that might be going on outside her door?

She couldn't think what it was that had woken her at five o'clock this cold, bleak, winter morning. Footsteps? The noise of rustling beneath her window? Someone clearing their throat? Or had all that been in her imagination?

It was no use. Now she was awake she just couldn't go back to sleep. Reaching for her dressing gown, she padded down the stairs. A quick peek outside, that's all she'd take, she decided, as she thrust back the bolt. Then, once her mind was at rest, she could get in a couple more hours at least before Lily-Rose started yelling for her breakfast.

At first, the shape was unrecognisable. Something big and bulky, wrapped in a bin bag. Then her eyes grew accustomed to the dark. There were two handles poking out, wound round with tinsel.

'What the . . . ?'

Carly put out a hand warily and tugged at it, marvelling at the silent way it glided towards her on silken wheels. Now it was in the house and she was tearing at the wrapping, desperate to see if her suspicions were correct.

When it was revealed to her in all its glory, she gasped, unable to believe her luck.

Someone had bought her her first Christmas present — a brand-new buggy!

# 2

Shelley was thinking about Guy and his new puppy, Dog, again. Guy patiently teaching Dog how to cross the road nicely. Dog rolling over on his back, relishing having his tummy tickled by the person he adored most in the whole world. Both of them simply revelling in each other's company by the fire in Guy's lounge, occasionally exchanging the fond glances of new lovers.

'Pull yourself together, Shelley. You can't be jealous of a dog, surely,' she told herself, as she pushed open the door of Rezia's Mini Mart one mild December morning. Maybe jealous was the wrong word, but lately she'd definitely started to feel a bit of a gooseberry.

Dog took orders from no one but his Lord and Master, as she'd found out on the three occasions she'd tried — and failed — to control him when it had been her turn to take him for a walk.

'He hates me,' she'd announced dramatically at breakfast that morning, when she remembered she'd agreed to take Dog out again later that afternoon.

'He's a dog, Mum. How can he hate you?' Nathan spoke through a mouthful of cereal. 'Stop anthropomorphising.'

Shelley was happy her son wasn't wasting his educational opportunities, but she hated it when he used words she didn't understand.

Unable to think of anything clever to say back, she resorted to telling Nathan not to talk with his mouth full, always a sure-fire way of restoring the balance of power in their relationship.

At Rezia's, Shelley's arrival put a sudden end to the discussion around the checkout. Feeling like the unwelcome stranger who walks into the bar in a Western, Shelley mustered a confident smile. She'd come here to speak to Rezia about the forged twenty-pound notes. Anything else that was going on was irrelevant. Until it became relevant, that was.

She knew everyone by sight, of course. A couple of mums eyed her warily, as well they might, given the long and chequered criminal history of their teenage sons. Rezia herself, resplendent in her ruby-red sari, jangled her gold bracelets. A shy-looking young girl Shelley's own daughter, Heather's, age, leaning against a buggy that took up a great deal of space and containing a smiley toddler, glanced at Shelley briefly, then quickly glanced away. And in the centre of all of it, surprise, surprise, was Josie Farlow.

Josie had been at school with Shelley and had bullied her remorselessly till the day she left. Now she was a single mum with several children and a partner serving time for GBH. Relations between Shelley and Josie had softened since Shelley had interceded between one of her sons and the law, but they were never going to be on each other's Christmas-card lists.

Taking as little time as duty permitted, Shelley checked that Rezia had had her promised visit from someone from the Fraud Squad. Then, with little more ado, she was on her way again. She knew when she wasn't welcome!

'I thought she'd never leave.' Josie Farlow's face was sour. 'Give people a uniform and it goes straight to their heads.'

The other women — Josie's cronies — sniffed in agreement. You didn't disagree with Josie Farlow. Carly said nothing either. But she'd gone to school with Heather and, though it didn't look like Shelley remembered her, Carly remembered Shelley from the times she'd been round to Heather's for birthday parties and to play as a child, and she'd always come across to her as really kind and generous.

'She's only doing her job.' Rezia said. 'We could do with more like her, if you ask me. Now, tell us again what happened when you opened your front door this morning, Carly.'

Carly retold the story she'd already told her mum, her nan and several friends she'd bumped into, all of whom expressed amazement at the sight of her expensive-looking buggy, which, to all intents and purposes, seemed brand new, apart from a tiny mark above one of the wheels.

Each time she told it, she couldn't help embellishing it slightly. Carly hadn't been the centre of attention since Year Eleven, when the news spread like wildfire through school that she was pregnant to Steve Robinson, and she was revelling in it.

She told them how she'd been woken by rustling sounds outside her door and footsteps running off, and how she'd decided to brave it and go downstairs to check out what was going on. She told them how surprised she'd been when she rolled the buggy inside and how she had absolutely no idea who would do such a kind thing. And she told them that if the buggy wasn't enough, whoever had decided to present her with this gift had topped it off with two extra presents, gift-wrapped and tucked inside the buggy.

'A gorgeous party dress for Lily-Rose, with tights and little shoes, and a dead expensive top for me!'

She didn't tell them of the hours she'd spent hoping that somehow it was Steve who was her anonymous benefactor — that he'd seen the error of his ways and this was his way of saying he wanted to get back with her. Though where he'd got the money to buy all this top-of-the-range stuff, she hadn't dared start thinking about.

'All you need is a party to go to.' Rezia smiled kindly.

Carly flushed. 'No chance,' she said. 'I never go out these days.'

'Well, you never know, maybe your luck's changing and this is just the start of it,' Rezia replied.

'Well, I wish my luck would change,' Josie grumbled. 'I've heard of a few other people who've had stuff shoved through their letter boxes. A mobile phone that takes videos and one of those iPods.'

'Then there was that lad who got his bike nicked and ended up with a new one costing twice as much,' one of the other women said.

'All I ever get through my door is final reminders,' Josie said glumly, before picking up her shopping bag with a heartfelt sigh.

⋆　⋆　⋆

Shelley was due a break. The sun had come out, it was her half-day, and she decided to take advantage of the mild air to cycle down to Quayside to say hello to Ruby, and to see if she'd thought about how she'd be spending Christmas.

It was a mere formality, of course, since her mother's houseboat was far too small to accommodate all Shelley's lot. This year there would be Guy, too, which she couldn't help being excited about. Although some of her excitement began to wear off when she realised he'd very probably insist on bringing Dog along.

Before Dog had bounded snuffling and barking on to the scene, she'd have said there was no contest. Guy longed for them to have more time alone and was forever trying to lure Shelley into his arms if he saw an opportunity, either at work or off duty. This past fortnight, though, he'd cancelled four times on her. Dog had to have his jab. He needed worming. It might be best if he took Dog out for a good long walk, so he could run off some of his exuberance. Anyone would think he was trying to dump her and was using Dog as an excuse.

'Hello, Starling! Come to arrest me, have you?'

If ever Shelley visited *Milarepa*, her mother's boat, in uniform, she could rely on Ruby trotting out the same old joke. It had long since ceased to irritate her, unlike her mother's habit of addressing her by the name on her birth certificate — the name she'd loathed from the moment her classmates had started flapping their arms and calling her Tweety Pie.

On her first day at secondary school, she'd announced that her name was Shelley but Ruby still clung to the name she'd bestowed on her daughter back in her hippy days.

'No. Just come to ask you what you're doing for Christmas.' Shelley ducked as she followed her mother inside.

'That's two reminders of Christmas I've had today already.'

Ruby's eyes sparkled with mischief, as she swept her arm theatrically over the huge festive food hamper taking pride of place on the galley table. Shelley's mouth dropped open in amazement.

'Have you won the Lottery or something? That must be worth two hundred at least!'

Greedily, her eyes took in the contents, Spiced Christmas coffee, at least two bottles of wine and one of port, Darjeeling tea, brandy butter, mince pies, chocolates, Christmas pudding — and that was only the stuff she could see.

'Came this morning,' Ruby said 'Fabulous, isn't it?'

Shelley was puzzled. Ruby's income was minuscule and she'd never been a spendthrift. She shopped by sell-by dates and never wore anything that didn't come from a thrift shop. Even the newspapers and magazines she read were second-hand ones that Shelley passed on.

Then something clicked. If she'd had her wits about her this morning, instead of wasting time obsessing about Dog and Guy, she might have got more of an inkling about the topic of conversation at Rezia's Mini Mart.

Could it have been the same topic of conversation she'd half-heard Heather and Nathan discussing while she'd been making a shopping list, boiling three eggs and wishing she hadn't promised Guy she'd take Dog out later, since she'd be finishing at lunchtime? They'd been talking about the paper boy who'd had a brand-new bike left outside his door. He had no idea who sent it, he'd said. Come to think of it, hadn't she seen the story in the paper herself?

She'd thought nothing of it then, other than it was a piece of good luck. But, this morning, Nathan had been telling Heather about rumours going round college. Something about the paper boy not being the only one. And Heather had cracked a joke about wishing whoever it was would leave her some new hair straighteners.

Was that what the women had been discussing this morning? Did they have knowledge of some other person who'd benefited? Not that discussing a crime was an offence, of course. And, if the person concerned was giving not taking, did that actually make what he was doing a crime?

Unless, of course, he was stealing the items in the first place. But if that was the case, why hadn't they been reported to the police as stolen? Or maybe they had, but Shelley just hadn't heard about it because they hadn't been stolen from her patch. The Burroway Estate housed mostly people on Income Support or with low-paid jobs. If they'd owned a top-of-the-range, five-speed racing bike, you could bet they hadn't come by it honestly, so they certainly wouldn't consider reporting its loss to the police.

'You didn't buy this, did you, Ruby?' Shelley dared her mother to try to wriggle out of it, with a look.

'I never said I had, did I? It was there, on the deck, when I opened the door earlier on this morning.'

'Did it have your name on it?'

'No! But if someone put it on my boat, then obviously it was meant for me.'

'It might be stolen property.' Shelley peered at the lid for evidence of an address. There was nothing. 'I should take it to the station. It might give the police some clue about who it is that's going round giving gifts to people.'

At this suggestion, Ruby put her foot down. She'd heard something about this anonymous Father Christmas, too, from rumours flying around the Quayside community, she said. So what if she'd benefited from it? Whoever it was obviously thought Ruby deserved a break. The only way Shelley would get the hamper out of the boat would be over her dead body.

Shelley had never been very good at standing up to her mother. Reluctantly, well aware her conscience would prick her badly for it, she agreed to keep it to herself. But Ruby had better not go around boasting about this, she said, and if she ever dared mention it to Guy, then Shelley would deny all knowledge that this conversation had ever taken place.

'What conversation?' Ruby asked sweetly. 'And how is Guy these days? Still favouring his new puppy over you?'

Ruby could be very astute. Had Shelley really given so much away about her feelings when she'd told Ruby of Guy's new acquisition?

'Come and help me walk it this afternoon,' she suggested. 'We could head out to Penniford Woods and look for cones to spray for Christmas decorations.'

Ruby smiled a self-satisfied smile.

'You mean you can't handle it on your own, then?' she said.

★ ★ ★

'So, Darius, no homework from you?'

Darius hated to see his language tutor, Jilly, disappointed. He felt as if he'd let her down. He wanted to explain fully, but he didn't have the English to tell Jilly everything in detail. That he'd truly meant to write his story — *An Unusual Event* — and that he'd known exactly what he intended to write and had started to plan it as soon as Jilly had given them the title, while the memory of his encounter with Carly and her broken buggy had still been fresh.

He'd even got pen and paper, dictionary and grammar book out. But then the music had started up again when Cosmo had turned up with several screeching girls and he'd simply abandoned all thoughts of doing anything other than getting under the duvet and pulling it over his head to block out the noise.

'You look tired, Darius,' Jilly said. 'You're late for school three days out of five and now you're getting behind on your homework. It's not good.'

'My house too noisy. I need quiet to study. I like to move but don't know how,' was what he said instead.

'Do you speak much English where you're living at the moment?'

Darius shook his head miserably.

'I wonder if you might be better with an English family. That way you'd get to practise your English every day.'

'But where I find?'

Jilly corrected him with a patient smile before suggesting he looked in the shop windows locally, where people wanting lodgers often advertised. In fact, now that she remembered, someone looking for a lodger had put an ad in her own mother's shop very recently.

'Your mother owns a shop?'

Darius was amazed at the thought of Jilly having a mother, let alone a life outside this school.

'Burton's,' she said. 'Bread and cakes. You know it?'

Darius grinned. 'Best cakes I tasted since my mother's,' he said.

'Flatterer,' Jilly chuckled. 'My mum'll love you! Go tonight and have a look on her noticeboard.'

A weight lifted from Darius's mind. Things might just work out for him in England after all, he thought, as he thanked Jilly for her advice and went back to his desk.

★ ★ ★

Carly was having mixed feelings about her new buggy. She was regretting blabbing about it in the shop the other day and she couldn't help worrying about Heather's mum. Perhaps she had recognised her after all, but was just pretending not to because she was in uniform and didn't want to embarrass Carly.

What if she'd mentioned to Heather that she'd seen her with a swish new buggy? It was only the other week Carly had bumped into her old schoolfriend in town and spent ages pointing out all the faults of her old one before going on to moan about having no money to replace it.

She told herself she was being paranoid. Heather's mum couldn't have recognised her. She was fourteen last time she'd been round there — maybe even younger. But if word got around — which it always did on this estate — then what would she tell the police about where her early Christmas present had come from? What could she tell them?

Ever since the buggy turned up on her doorstep she'd been racking her brain trying to work out who'd want to do her a good turn. Neither Mum nor Nan could lay their hands on twenty quid between them — and if they did, knowing their luck it'd be one of those forgeries that was going about the estate. As for Steve, she'd discounted him after bumping into his sister, who told her — with great relish because she'd never liked Carly — that he'd gone up to Scotland to see some girl.

There was one person whose face she couldn't seem to shift, though. Every time she looked at the buggy — which was a hundred times a day at least, since it was stuck in the corner of her living room — she remembered that foreign student who'd helped her get home the day the old buggy broke. Good-looking, right enough, but a bit creepy now she came to think of it. Never smiled. Just stared at her, like he'd never seen a woman before.

Carly shivered at the memory. What if he'd taken a shine to her and spent all his money on this buggy as a way of getting to her through Lily-Rose? Men did that sort of thing, she knew. But why hadn't he followed it up? After all, he had her address.

Suddenly there was a sharp rap on her front door. Carly froze, her heart pounded. Silently she crept upstairs and into her bedroom. Drawing aside the curtain, she peered out on to the street.

It was him! And it was no use pretending she wasn't in because he'd seen her and now he was waving at her.

She left the chain on as, with trembling fingers, she half-opened the door.

'I come for room,' he said, waving the postcard she'd pinned up on Eileen

Burton's noticeboard.

Oh, my God! What was she supposed to do now? There was no way she could let this person inside. He was a stalker, obviously. Why hadn't she seen the signs?

'Sorry, the room's gone,' she said.

Then, slamming the door in his face, she threw her full weight behind it and waited for her heart to still.

★　★　★

It had been a huge relief to let Dog off the lead once they'd finally arrived at Penniford Woods. En route, he'd practically wrenched Shelley's arm out of its socket and she was exhausted. She'd been looking forward to a bit of a breather now she'd finally got some feeling back in it. But now Dog was lost and she was panicking.

Ruby was no help at all, trailing behind, picking up twigs and leaves like some ancient Ophelia in red wellies. Shelley was just about ready to kill her, having been forced to put up with Ruby's supercilious expression that suggested she was an expert on how to handle a dog, but thought Shelley might benefit from the practice.

'Where can he have got to? It's like he suddenly caught the scent of something and bolted.'

Shelley suspected they'd been along this track before, but she was getting desperate.

'Probably smelled a rat,' Ruby said. 'Chill out, Shelley.'

'All right for you, Mother,' Shelley growled. 'You're not the one who has to face Guy and tell him his precious hound's gone missing.'

A volley of shrill barks suddenly rent the air.

'Dog!' Shelley yelled.

'This way!' Ruby cried out, forging a path through the undergrowth with a stick she'd found somewhere.

The two women followed Dog's manic barking, stumbling over the uneven ground as they did so. Shelley prayed that dogs were like babies in that if they were able to make such an ear-splitting racket there could be nothing really wrong with them.

Shelley saw the man first. Squatting on the ground, clutching his ankle and moaning with pain. Dog, ecstatic that he'd come across another human that bore a much closer resemblance to Guy than the two specimens who'd dragged him out on this walk — albeit a much scruffier and bedraggled version and one with a choice line in expletives — licked the man's face enthusiastically.

'Are you all right, sir?'

Shelley ran towards him. His shoe had come off, revealing a sock that was more hole than material.

'Just call your dog off!' The man's voice was muffled, coming as it did from beneath Dog's large and exuberant frame.

She was just about to do so when something else caught Shelley's eye. Some distance away, a black nylon holdall had spilled its contents on to the ground. At first, she thought she was imagining what she saw. Excitedly, she scrambled over to the bag and bent down to retrieve one of the bundles from the ground. What a spot of luck! And it was all down to Dog. Guy would be thrilled beyond belief when this piece of news got back to him.

'I don't think I'll be calling him off just yet, sir. Not till the police get here, anyway.' Turning to Ruby, she cried out, 'Catch, Mum. Looks like Dog here has caught the forger.'

Ruby positioned herself to catch the bundle of notes as it winged its way towards her in a perfect arc, whistling in amazement as she caught it expertly.

# 3

This shopping expedition had been the idea of Shelley's daughter, Heather. After all, it wasn't every day you won an award and got to shake the hand of the Chief Constable, she said. A new dress was the very least Shelley should be planning to invest in if she wanted to do herself justice on the front cover of the local paper.

Strictly speaking, it was Dog who'd won the award, drenching the recumbent forger in a torrent of unrestrained doggy kisses till the police turned up to arrest him, prior to transporting him to A&E for X-rays on his shattered ankle.

It was the old tale of greed, so Shelley later learned from the Duty Officer. Ron Smiley, who, as the brains of the counterfeiting operation, had been unwilling to budge on percentages, had driven Duggie Baron, who possessed the brawn, to finally make a break with Smiley — taking with him as many notes as would fit into his holdall.

On the afternoon of his unfortunate encounter with Dog and Shelley, he'd been heading away from the ramshackle hut deep in the heart of Penniford Wood which housed their business operation, presumably celebrating the fact that even if Smiley and he were now at the end of the road, Baron had succeeded in grabbing more than enough loot to see him through till his next business opportunity came up.

Unfortunately, he met his nemesis in the shape of Dog, who, offended at having his affections spurned, decided to pursue Baron until he changed his mind. A terrified Baron — whose long-standing fear of dogs stemmed from a childhood incident when he'd been set upon by the Alsatian belonging to the owners of the property he'd been attempting to break into — had fled, tripping over the root of a tree, falling heavily and spilling his booty all over the ground, which was where Shelley and Ruby had discovered him.

Shelley hated clothes shopping but she loved spending time with Heather, so she'd jumped at the opportunity. The fact was, she'd been fretting too much over Guy and his intentions recently and everybody else in her life had dropped right off the bottom of her list. She loved him, yes — her anxiety over her fears of Dog usurping his affections had proved that to her. Recently, she'd been daring to hope he loved her in return.

For one thing, his pride in her part in Dog's recent adventure was evident for all to see. More importantly, Shelley had convinced herself there'd been a shift in the balance of his affections. The initially unruly Dog was now, thanks to Guy, perfectly behaved. Perhaps all Guy had ever really wanted from Dog was to get him to calm down a bit and the fault had lain with Shelley for resenting the time he needed to put in, in order for his efforts to succeed.

Now, watching Heather spoon foam from her cappuccino into her mouth as she chattered on about life at college, in the Italian coffee bar just off the high street, Shelley allowed all thoughts of Guy and Dog and criminals to drift away. This was Heather's time.

Heather was talking about Carly.

'Remember her, Mum? Got stuck with that loser, Steve Robinson? Got a little girl, Lily-Rose? Dead cute!'

'Vaguely.' Shelley was loath to admit that she often confused Heather's friends since, as well as her having so many, Shelley rarely got to see them for longer than five minutes at a time before Heather dragged them off up to her room, or out of the house altogether.

'Saw her in town the other week. Complaining about her buggy being on its last legs and having no money to replace it.'

Shelley racked her brains. 'Did she used to come to your parties when you were younger? Fair-haired? A bit plump?'

'No! Skinny! Dark hair. We sort of drifted apart somewhere around the middle of Year Nine. Like you do.'

'I think I remember her,' Shelley said unconvincingly.

'No, you don't, Mum, so stop pretending.' Heather grinned. 'Now, if you've finished, there's this ultra-cool boutique down Bridge Street.'

As well as being ultra-cool, it quickly

became apparent that the shop was also ultra-expensive. Which might have accounted for the fact that the shop was empty apart from its owner, an elegant thirty-something woman, who, without ungluing her phone from her ear, glanced up to greet them with a faux-friendly smile before immediately returning to the conversation she clearly thought much more interesting.

It always amazed Shelley how much personal stuff people revealed on their phones. She was curious by nature, but you could hardly call it eavesdropping if people couldn't wait till they were alone to share their latest gossip with a friend.

'I suppose I'm just going to have to put it down to experience,' the woman drawled. 'Honestly, Camilla, I only turned my back for two seconds, because Jamie said that if she didn't get out of her buggy and on to her potty immediately then . . . well, you know what it's like with two-year-olds.'

Shelley selected a dove-grey silk top she thought might go with her black velvet trousers, gasped at the price and put it back.

'Two minutes! That was all, I swear. But when I came back outside it had vanished! I don't know what Beaulieu Road's coming to, Camilla, seriously. There are always pushbikes disappearing from people's lawns. Plus my next-door neighbour had a hamper stolen from outside her house the other day. Can you believe it?'

Shelley felt the blood pumping in her ears. Disappearing bikes. Stolen buggies. This was all beginning to sound remarkably familiar. And with the mention of the hamper it had suddenly got personal. Shelley grabbed a red dress from the rail without even bothering to glance at the price tag. She'd no intention of buying it, but she'd try on the entire stock if it meant she had a chance of learning more about the thefts from — where was it? — Beaulieu Road. At the other end of town and as far removed from the Burroway Estate as this dress was from anything hanging in Shelley's wardrobe.

She signalled her intentions of trying it on and the woman on the phone pointed to the fitting room, without missing a beat of her exchange with the invisible Camilla.

With her ear to the curtain, Shelley strained to hear more.

'Robert? No, not furious, exactly. Said we should just claim on the insurance. That way we can upgrade. Jamie's buggy was already practically a year old anyway — I know, ancient! They've brought out a much cooler model since.'

Honestly, some people had more money than sense! Shelley's thoughts turned to that girl, Carly, who Heather had mentioned and whose face still escaped her. A buggy on its last legs and no money with which to replace it.

And then, like a light going on inside her head, she saw Carly standing right in front of her, at Rezia's. Now she remembered her. Dark-haired, skinny, just as Heather had described her. And with a buggy the size of a house that, to all intents and purposes seemed brand new to the casual onlooker.

Shelley ran her fingers over the red

dress on the hanger and ruminated on everything she'd heard so far. When she drew back the curtain, Heather was admiring a bright-orange taffeta party dress.

'Not your colour,' Shelley hissed, slotting the red dress back where she'd found it. 'Don't know about you, but I need to get out of here.'

Mobile-phone Woman was still at it, even as Shelley and Heather turned to mouth goodbye.

''Course, I didn't dare mention *that* to Robert. I'd promised I wouldn't buy another outfit either for me or Jamie till the sales,' she said. 'But then I popped into Supermums. I *know*. Three hundred pounds wiped off my credit card and nothing to show for it.'

'She didn't even notice we'd gone, stuck-up cow,' Heather said, as she shut the door behind them.

Shelley's mobile bleeped. A message from Guy.

'Anything interesting?'

Shelley grinned. 'He wants to know why I'm shopping for a new outfit.'

'Nathan must have told him,' Heather

said. 'What's so funny?'

Shelley read the rest of Guy's message out loud.

'*All presentations done in full uniform*, it says.'

Heather pulled a disappointed face. 'What! You're going to have to be in the newspaper in uniform? How grim is that!'

Shelley longed to get back to Burroway but she'd promised to spend the day with Heather, so her plans would simply have to wait. Tomorrow she'd pay Carly a visit — find out if Father Christmas had left her a designer outfit or two along with that buggy. And that was just for starters.

Someone should pay a visit to the residents of Beaulieu Road to see if what Shelley had just heard about the bikes and the hamper could be backed up. Though what on earth she was going to do about the fact that her own mother was in possession of stolen goods, she had no idea.

'Come on!' Shelley put her arm through Heather's, determined not to dwell on it. 'Since I no longer need a new dress, I'll treat you.'

* * *

Shelley sat in Carly's cluttered living room. Every now and then Lily-Rose toddled over and offered her one of her toys. Right now, Shelley was pretending to drink tea from a red plastic cup.

For the first ten minutes of their conversation at least, Shelley and Carly had been talking at cross-purposes. Shelley was here unofficially, to find out a little bit more about how Carly had come by the buggy that took pride of place in the middle of her living room and to find out if what she suspected was true — that Carly's benefactor had also left a couple of designer outfits, one for Carly and one for Lily-Rose.

But now this other incident with the male student had come to light. Carly seemed genuinely afraid as she explained how she'd been visited not once, but twice, by the same boy she'd initially looked upon as kind and thoughtful for helping her home with her shopping when the wheel of her old buggy dropped off.

But when a brand-new buggy appeared on her step less than a week later, she began to suspect that he must have bought it for her, as a way of getting at her through Lily-Rose.

'Except now I find out it's not brand new,' Carly said. 'So not only is he stalking me but he's about to get me nicked for receiving.'

'Please, Carly. You mustn't worry about the buggy. You say he's tried to get you to let him inside the house on two other occasions since the first time he came round to look at the room you advertised?'

'That's right. Only the last time he came knocking on my door I got his picture, didn't I?' Carly brandished her phone triumphantly. 'So I want you to go after him, find him and press charges.'

★   ★   ★

Ianthe had been droning on about her mother ever since they'd got out of school. God, she could be so *boring*. Everything was boring these days. Nothing but coursework and coming home early at weekends and parents going on about GCSEs, when they weren't going on about him losing his iPod and his iPhone, which he hadn't lost, *actually*, just put down somewhere in the house and now he couldn't find them.

That wasn't good enough for his dad, though, who was never one to miss a chance to get at him. *What about your bike, then? Put that down somewhere and can't find that either, did you? Blah blah blah.* Like it was Tom's fault if someone comes along and steals it from the garage. If his father was that bothered about losing things, then he should get CCTV installed. Anyway, that bike was rubbish. He was glad someone had taken it. Now he could get a better one on the insurance.

'You haven't been listening to a word I've said, have you?' Ianthe whined, as they turned into Beaulieu Road. 'Thinking about Yummy Mummy at number 36 again, I bet. Like she'd look at you, *little boy.*'

Tom protested that he wasn't remotely interested in the woman who lived opposite, but he knew Ianthe could see right through him. Girls were like that. How did they notice so much stuff while they were doing other things at the same time — mostly *talking*, in his experience? He'd never understand.

Perhaps he should be nicer to Ianthe. She had a party coming up next month and he'd look a right loser if he was the only one in the class not to get an invitation.

'You were complaining about your mother again,' he said. 'And something about a Christmas hamper disappearing off your step and you getting blamed for it.'

'So you were listening, then,' Ianthe said, batting her eyelids in a frightening manner.

By the time they'd reached her house, she'd got to the end of her tedious tale, the delivery man ringing the bell just as Ianthe was letting herself out to go to school, Ianthe's mother shrieking down the stairs at her to go and sign for it because she was still in bed.

'Then *ordering* me to bring it inside

and not to leave it on the step! Like, didn't she know if I was late again I'd get detention?'

'So you left it there, huh?'

Tom kicked the ground.

'Too right. What did her last slave die of? Hardly my fault she's too hung over to get out of bed and pick it up herself, is it?' Then, without missing a beat, she said, 'Coming to mine? We could watch a DVD.'

'Nah! Got extra English.'

Ianthe grimaced. ''Course, if you'd asked me for help I could have spared you the ordeal of having to have a tutor.'

'Yeah, whatever, Ianthe,' Tom growled, as he opened the gate to his house. 'See you tomorrow, swot-face.'

Ianthe waited for Tom to disappear inside. He definitely fancied her.

★ ★ ★

Darius stood on the steps of the Police Station, breathing in the fresh air — a free man at last. It wasn't true what they said about England. You could still be arrested, even here, just because people didn't like the look of you.

All he'd wanted was a chance to talk to Carly and to find out why she'd refused to open the door to him when he went to ask her about the room. But she'd called the police. Said he was harassing her. And now he'd been told he mustn't go anywhere near her home or he would be arrested.

Darius stared up at the sky. Already it was dark. He shivered in his thin jacket. Soon, term would be at an end and he'd be going home for Christmas. Only yesterday, Jilly Burton, his English teacher, had asked him if he'd be returning in January because, if so, he needed to re-register by the end of the week.

He'd answered vaguely. It depended, though, on what he hadn't said. If things got better in the house, if he made friends, if people started to accept him. Well, none of this was going to happen. Not in England, not for him. No, he wouldn't be re-registering. He'd tell Jilly so tomorrow. And then he'd let his mother know that he was coming home for good.

* * *

Shelley and Guy were going through all the information that the house-to-house on Beaulieu Road had thrown up. Shelley had popped into Burton's on her way back from Rezia's, who'd been so delighted to discover the forgers were in custody that she'd donated ten pounds to the Police Benevolent Christmas Fund.

Now Shelley and Guy were munching their way amicably through their first mince pies of the season. Every now and then, Dog would look up from his position as a doorstop and give a complaining whine. But he knew better now than to hope for any crumbs.

'None of this stuff has been reported as stolen, have you noticed?' Guy said. 'Not even the bike. Apparently, the son of the house loses things with tedious regularity. They just get a new one on the insurance and put it down to experience.'

An exact replica of what Mobile-phone Woman had said about her buggy, Shelley mused.

'And this luxury hamper. Woman said

she got on the phone to complain and they sent her another round within three days.'

Shelley was mightily relieved about that. She hated keeping Ruby's involvement in the hamper scam from Guy, but what would be the point of involving him? He was a policeman through and through, and if he found out that she was certain, he'd demand Ruby present herself and her unlawfully acquired hamper to the nearest police station immediately. Ruby would refuse to do so, call Guy a righteous prig, and then Shelley would feel awkward. And all just in time for Christmas, which would make for a great Christmas dinner.

'Anyway, Sherlock,' Guy said, brushing the mince-pie crumbs away as he stood up, 'I'll love you and leave you.'

'Where you off to, then?'

Guy tapped the side of his nose.

'Top secret,' he said, with a grin. 'See you when we get back. Come on, Dog. Walkies!'

It was probably just some boring meeting, Shelley thought, once she was alone. Guy's attempt to inject a note of mystery was his way of pretending to her that his job still held enough glamour for him to get through the day.

'I'm not convinced, though,' Shelley said aloud, before turning her thoughts back to Beaulieu Road.

Shelley stared at the page before her. These people had everything. The recipients of the same goods had had nothing. The deserving poor, they used to be called, in the olden days. It was like Robin Hood all over again, Shelley mused.

The boy from the paper shop had got a new bike, which meant he got his round back. The story of the theft had been in the paper, so anyone could have read that and decided to put it right.

But who had decided that Ruby — good-natured and always a soft touch for anyone down on their luck among her community of boat-dwellers — was worthy of such a luxurious hamper? And who would have known about Carly's broken buggy? The police had already discounted the foreign student, and the Beaulieu Road area of town might as well have been in China for its accessibility to Carly's friends and family.

Shelley glanced across at the bag that had contained the mince pies. The words *Burton's Bakery* stared up at her. Carly had posted her advert there, hadn't she? Maybe eagle-eyed Eileen, as the school kids called her, had noticed someone suspicious.

Shelley had got to know the owner of the baker's quite well from the occasions she'd popped into her shop for a sausage roll or a custard slice, so she'd be bound to want to help if she could. They both had daughters in common and had spoken about them at great length. Shelley remembered being surprised that Eileen's daughter, although a graduate, chose to 'slum it on a boat', according to her mother, and didn't want a proper job because it interfered with her charity work, something else that failed to impress her.

Shelley let the page drop from her fingers. Things were starting to slot into place. She was beginning to believe that she'd discovered Burroway's Robin Hood.

The photograph of Dog and Shelley receiving their award was Dog's very own Christmas present to her, according to Guy. He was looking really good in the blue cashmere sweater that had been her present to him — relaxed as he poured wine for everyone at the table on Christmas Day. After Christmas, he'd start his new job as dog handler — the job he'd kept secret from Shelley until he'd heard he'd been successful.

The day of his interview had been the day Jilly Burton had been arrested and charged with taking various items from the grounds and houses of Beaulieu Road. She'd confessed readily and with gusto. As tutor to Tom Palmer, she'd simply slipped his iPod into her bag one week when he'd had his back turned, and his iPhone into her pocket the following week.

She knew people much more deserving of them, she told the officer interviewing her, and anyway, it was hardly stealing, was it, if those from whom she'd taken the things thought nothing of fiddling their insurance and making claims for new ones?

She'd noticed the buggy in front of number 36 as she'd left Tom's after a lesson one afternoon. Her mother had told her about poor Carly's decrepit buggy, just as she'd told her about the paperboy who'd lost his job. And everyone on Quayside knew how generous Ruby was with her stuff, even though she existed on a pension. It was about time she got something in return.

Her story had been splashed over all the nationals, highlighting the plight of the social divide in the UK, and although Jilly Burton was now awaiting trial, for some on the Burroway Estate she was a local heroine.

'Trust Ruby to take up her cause,' Shelley thought, as her mother lifted her glass and, mischievously, proposed a toast to Jilly.

'You're incorrigible, Grandmother,' Nathan said.

Shelley rolled her eyes at Guy, who just sat at the table grinning. If Ruby wanted to pick a fight, then it was no use starting on Guy. He didn't seem to be listening.

'I think we should toast Gran,' Heather said. 'After all, she did give the contents of her hamper to the old people's home.'

'Really? I didn't know that!'

'What else could I have done,' Ruby said, 'with a PCSO for a daughter and a police-officer-till-next-month for a . . . '

A sudden hush descended on the table and Shelley felt her colour rise. She didn't know where to look! Somehow, she was going to have to find the opportunity later to apologise to Guy for her mother's interference in their lives.

'I was just about to get to that, Ruby, but thanks for the hint, anyway.'

Guy had risen from the table and was on his way round to Shelley. What was going on?

'Shelley,' he said. 'I know you must have been wondering all day where my present to you was.'

'Oh, I . . . '

Shelley felt flustered. Why was everyone staring at her? And what on earth was Guy doing, going down on one knee?